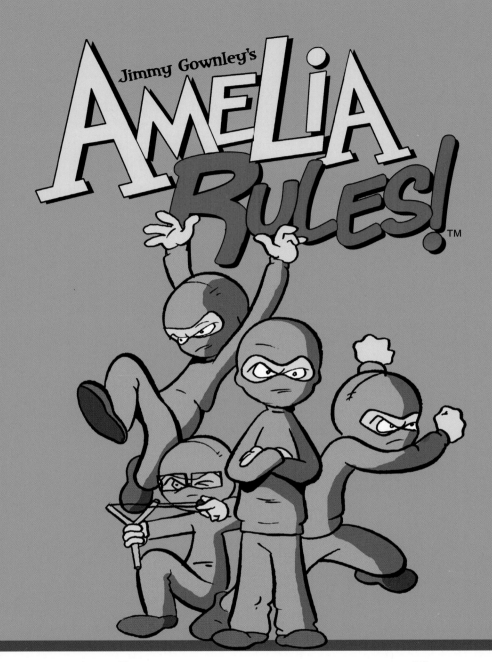

Jimmy Gownley's AMELIA RULES!™

Heroes and Villains

Atheneum Books for Young Readers
New York London Toronto

Spotlight

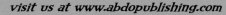

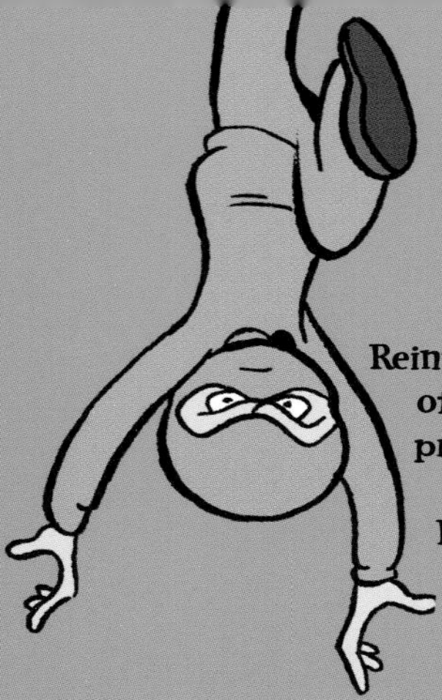

visit us at www.abdopublishing.com

Reinforced library bound edition published in 2013 by Spotlight, a division of the ABDO Group, PO Box 398166, Minneapolis, MN 55439. Spotlight produces high-quality reinforced library bound editions for schools and libraries. Published by agreement with Atheneum Books for Young Readers, an imprint of Simon & Schuster Children's Publishing Division.

Printed in the United States of America, North Mankato, Minnesota.
102012
012013
This book contains at least 10% recycled materials.

· Special thanks to Michael Cohen ·

Book design by Jimmy Gownley and Sonia Chaghatzbanian

Library of Congress Cataloging-in-Publication Data

Gownley, Jimmy.
Amelia in heroes and villains / [Jimmy Gownley]. -- Reinforced library bound ed.
p. cm. -- (Jimmy Gownley's Amelia rules!)
Summary: After a shared homework assignment goes awry, Rhonda and Amelia figure out why they are always fighting, while "superhero" Reggie and "ninja" Kyle try to become archenemies.
ISBN 978-1-61479-070-9
[1. Graphic novels. 2. Friendship--Fiction. 3. Enemies--Fiction.] I. Title.
PZ7.7.G69Amk 2013
741.5'973--dc23

2012026909

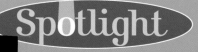

Spotlight

[redacted] books are reinforced library bindings
[redacted]ctured in the United States of America.

To my beautiful girls:
Stella Mary and
Anna Elizabeth,
And to their wonderful mother, Karen.

You're what make ME happy.

MEET THE GANG

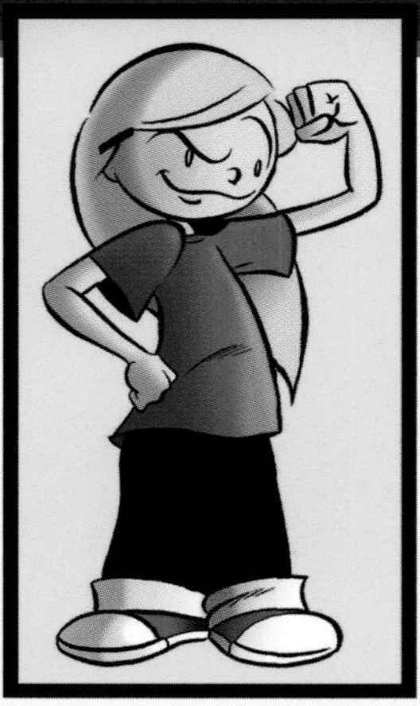

Amelia Louise McBride:
Our heroine. Wise cracking, yet sweet. She spends her time hanging out with friends and her aunt Tanner.

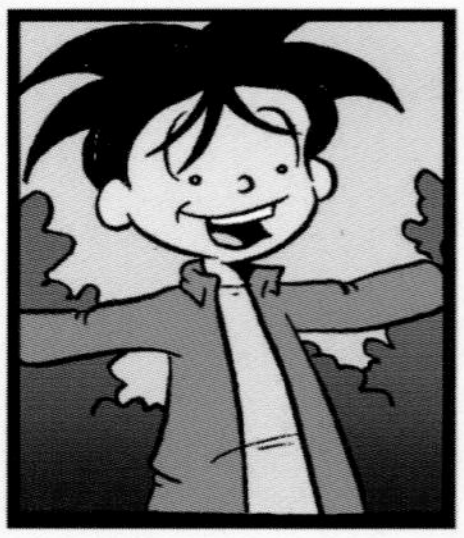

Reggie Grabinsky:
A.k.a. Captain Amazing. Founder of G.A.S.P., which he forces . . . er, encourages, his friends to join.

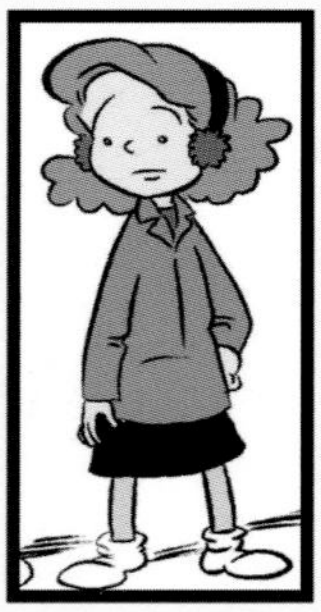

Rhonda Bleenie:
Smart, stubborn, and loud. She wears her heart on her sleeve and it's filled with love for Reggie.

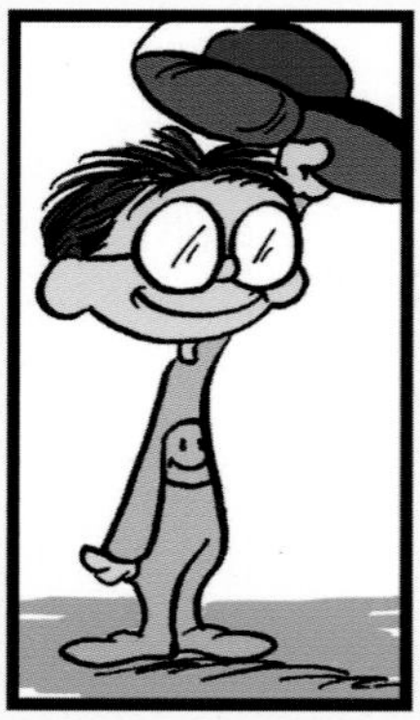

Pajamaman:
Never speaks. Always cool. His feetie jammies tell you what's on his mind.

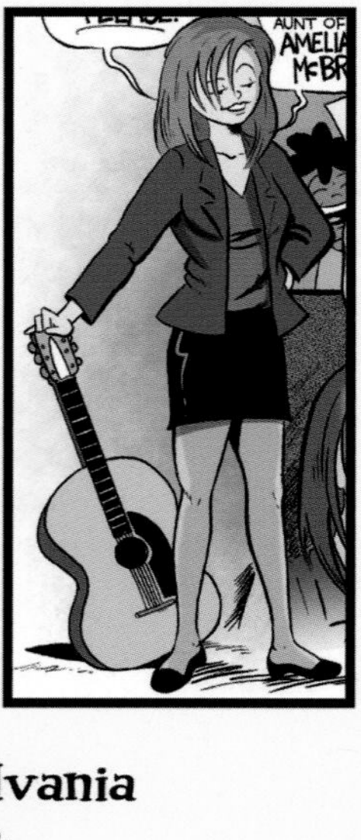
AUNT OF AMELIA

Tanner:
Amelia's aunt and a former rock 'n' roll superstar.

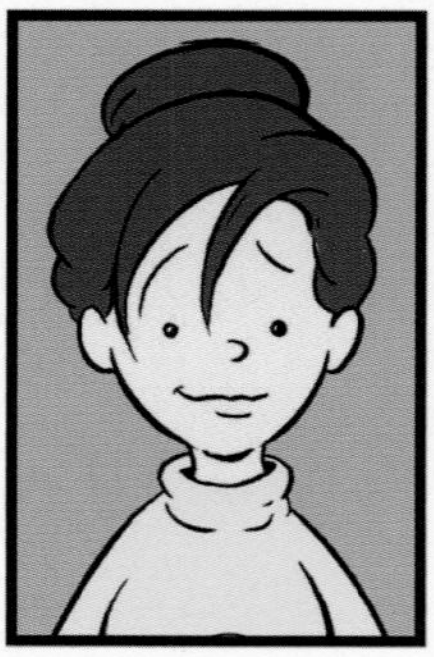

Amelia's Mom (Mary):
Starting a new life in Pennsylvania with Amelia after the divorce.

Amelia's Dad:
Still lives in New York, and misses Amelia terribly.

G.A.S.P.
Gathering Of Awesome Super Pals. The superhero club Reggie founded.

Park View Terrace Ninjas:
Club across town and nemesis to G.A.S.P.

Kyle:
The main ninja. Kind of a jerk but not without charm.

Joan:
Former Park View Terrace Ninja (nemesis of G.A.S.P.), now friends with Amelia and company.

Tweenie Zeenie:
A local kid-run magazine and Web site.

tweeniezeenie.com

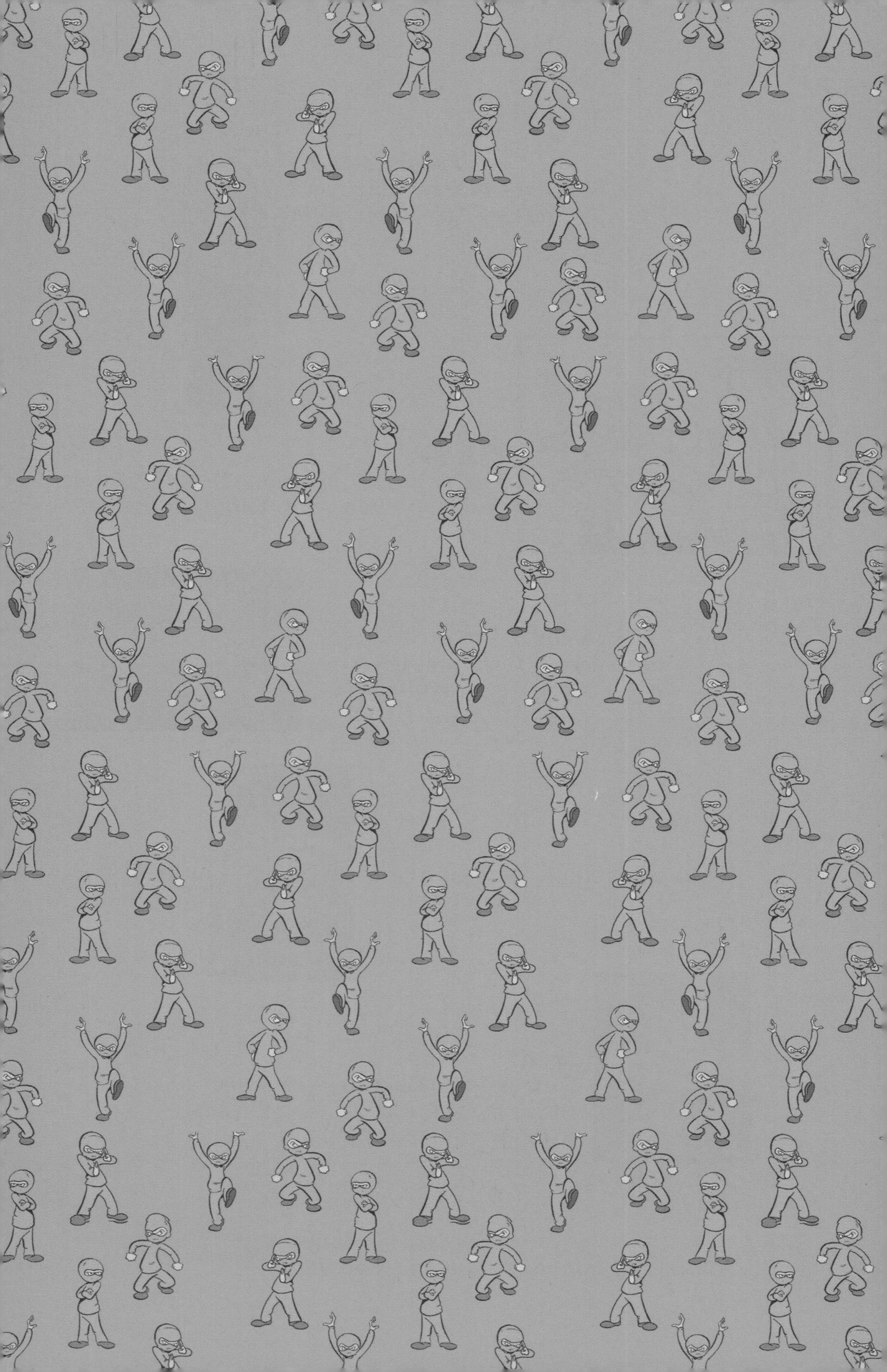

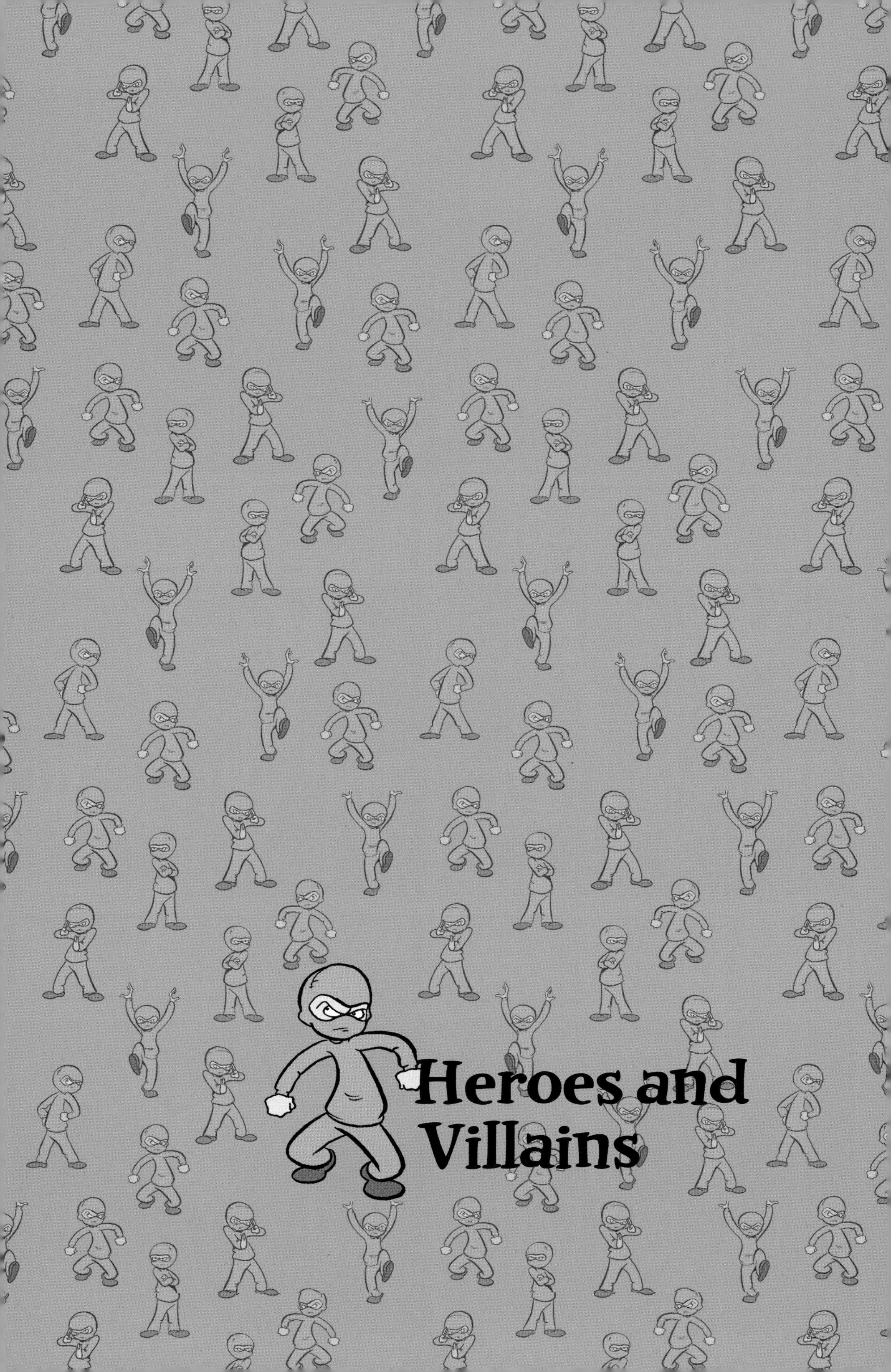

Heroes and Villains

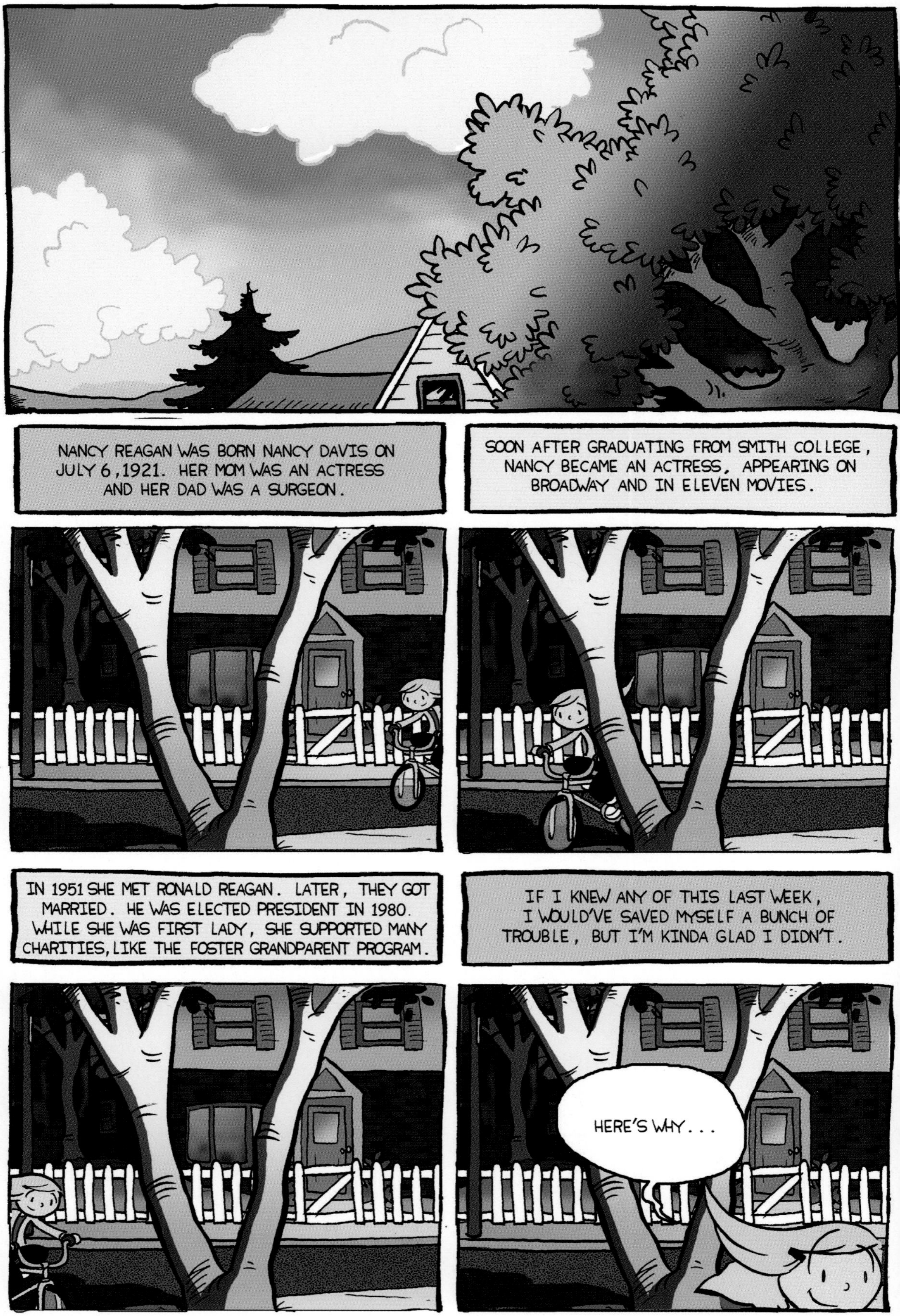
NANCY REAGAN WAS BORN NANCY DAVIS ON JULY 6, 1921. HER MOM WAS AN ACTRESS AND HER DAD WAS A SURGEON.
SOON AFTER GRADUATING FROM SMITH COLLEGE, NANCY BECAME AN ACTRESS, APPEARING ON BROADWAY AND IN ELEVEN MOVIES.
IN 1951 SHE MET RONALD REAGAN. LATER, THEY GOT MARRIED. HE WAS ELECTED PRESIDENT IN 1980. WHILE SHE WAS FIRST LADY, SHE SUPPORTED MANY CHARITIES, LIKE THE FOSTER GRANDPARENT PROGRAM.
IF I KNEW ANY OF THIS LAST WEEK, I WOULD'VE SAVED MYSELF A BUNCH OF TROUBLE, BUT I'M KINDA GLAD I DIDN'T.
HERE'S WHY . . .

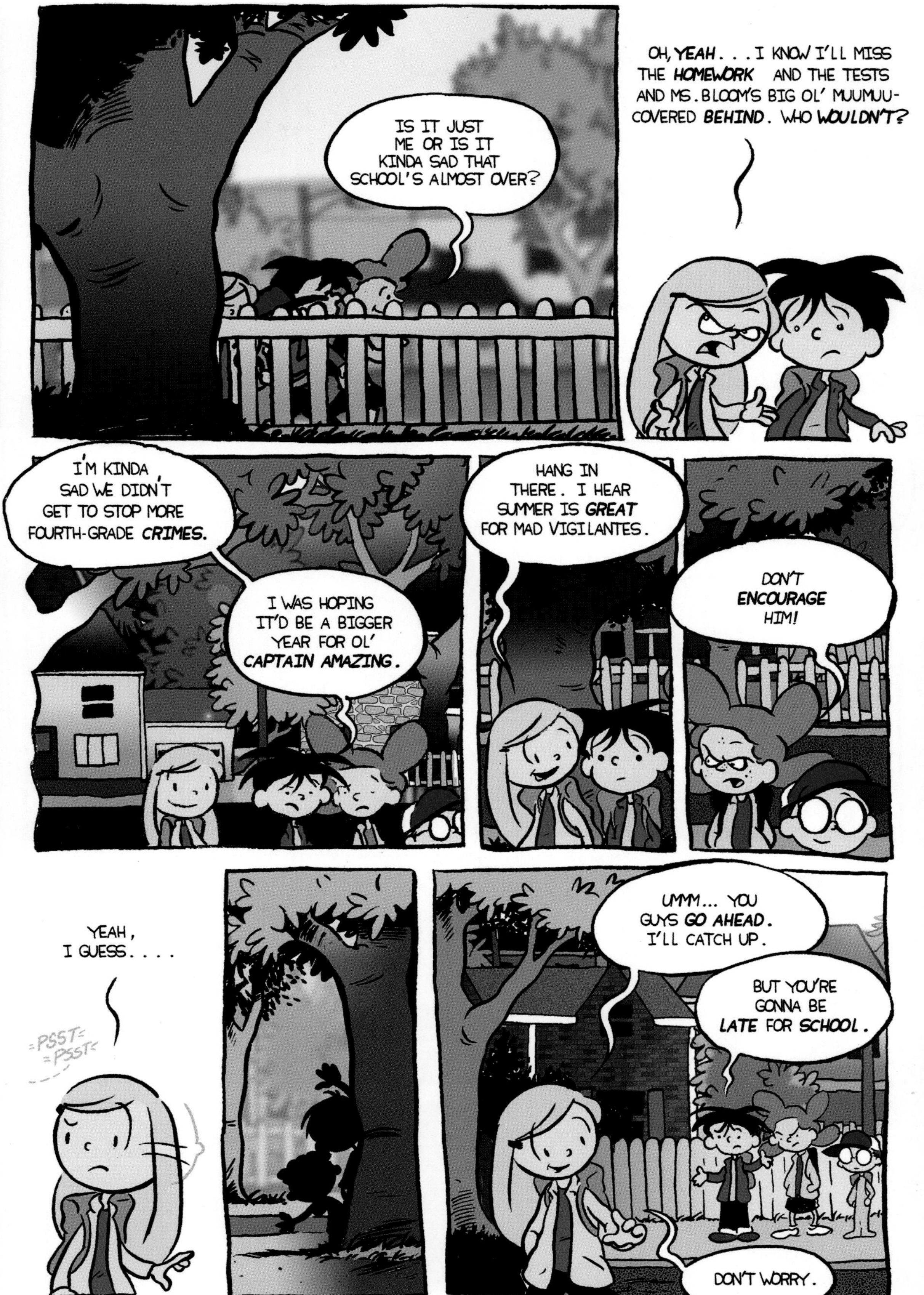
IS IT JUST ME OR IS IT KINDA SAD THAT SCHOOL'S ALMOST OVER?
OH, YEAH . . . I KNOW I'LL MISS THE HOMEWORK AND THE TESTS AND MS. BLOOM'S BIG OL' MUUMUU-COVERED BEHIND. WHO WOULDN'T?
I'M KINDA SAD WE DIDN'T GET TO STOP MORE FOURTH-GRADE CRIMES.
I WAS HOPING IT'D BE A BIGGER YEAR FOR OL' CAPTAIN AMAZING.
HANG IN THERE. I HEAR SUMMER IS GREAT FOR MAD VIGILANTES.
DON'T ENCOURAGE HIM!
YEAH, I GUESS. . . .
=PSST=
=PSST=
UMMM... YOU GUYS GO AHEAD. I'LL CATCH UP.
BUT YOU'RE GONNA BE LATE FOR SCHOOL.
DON'T WORRY.

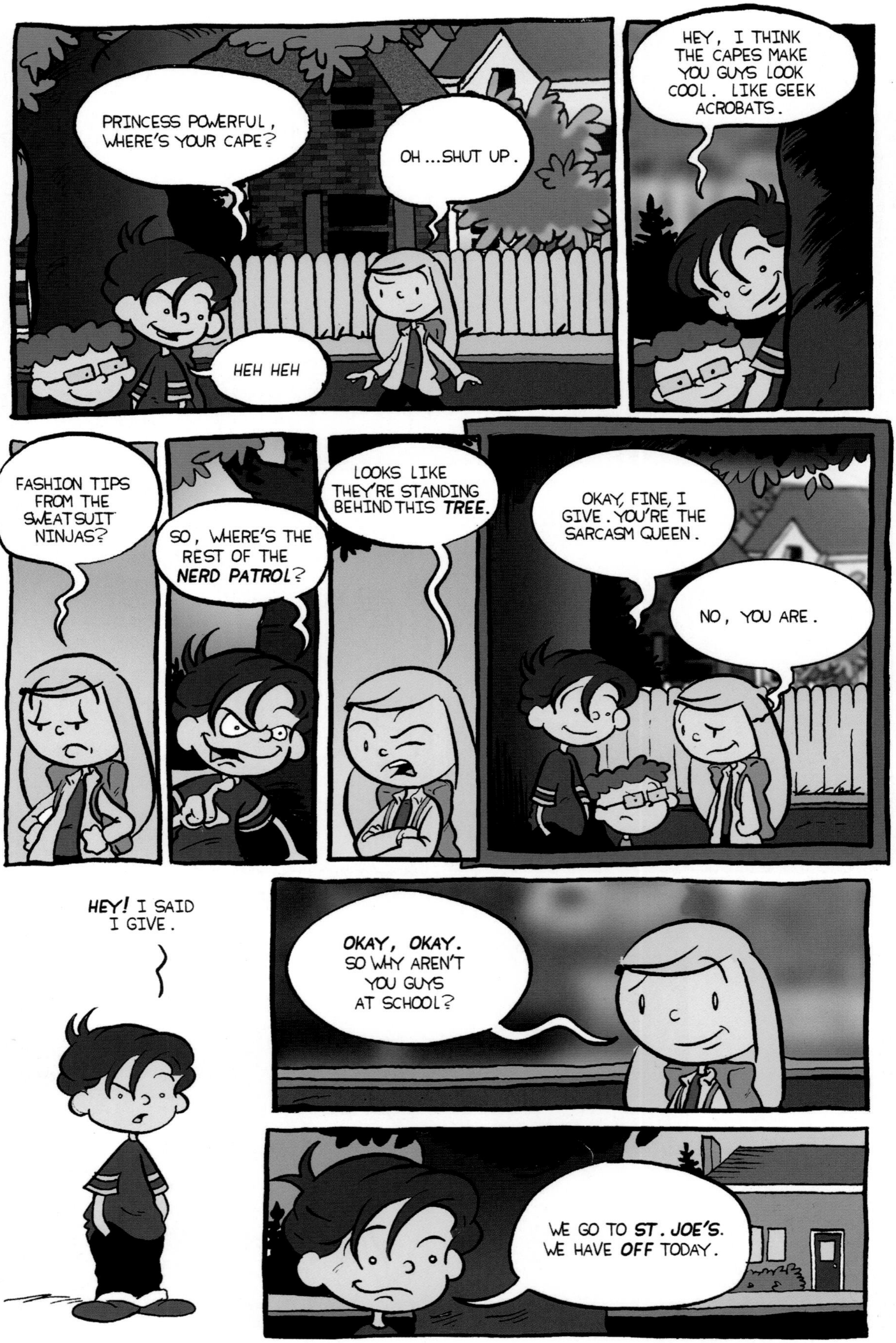

PRINCESS POWERFUL, WHERE'S YOUR CAPE?
OH ...SHUT UP.
HEH HEH
HEY, I THINK THE CAPES MAKE YOU GUYS LOOK COOL. LIKE GEEK ACROBATS.
FASHION TIPS FROM THE SWEATSUIT NINJAS?
SO, WHERE'S THE REST OF THE NERD PATROL?
LOOKS LIKE THEY'RE STANDING BEHIND THIS TREE.
OKAY, FINE, I GIVE. YOU'RE THE SARCASM QUEEN.
NO, YOU ARE.
HEY! I SAID I GIVE.
OKAY, OKAY. SO WHY AREN'T YOU GUYS AT SCHOOL?
WE GO TO ST. JOE'S. WE HAVE OFF TODAY.

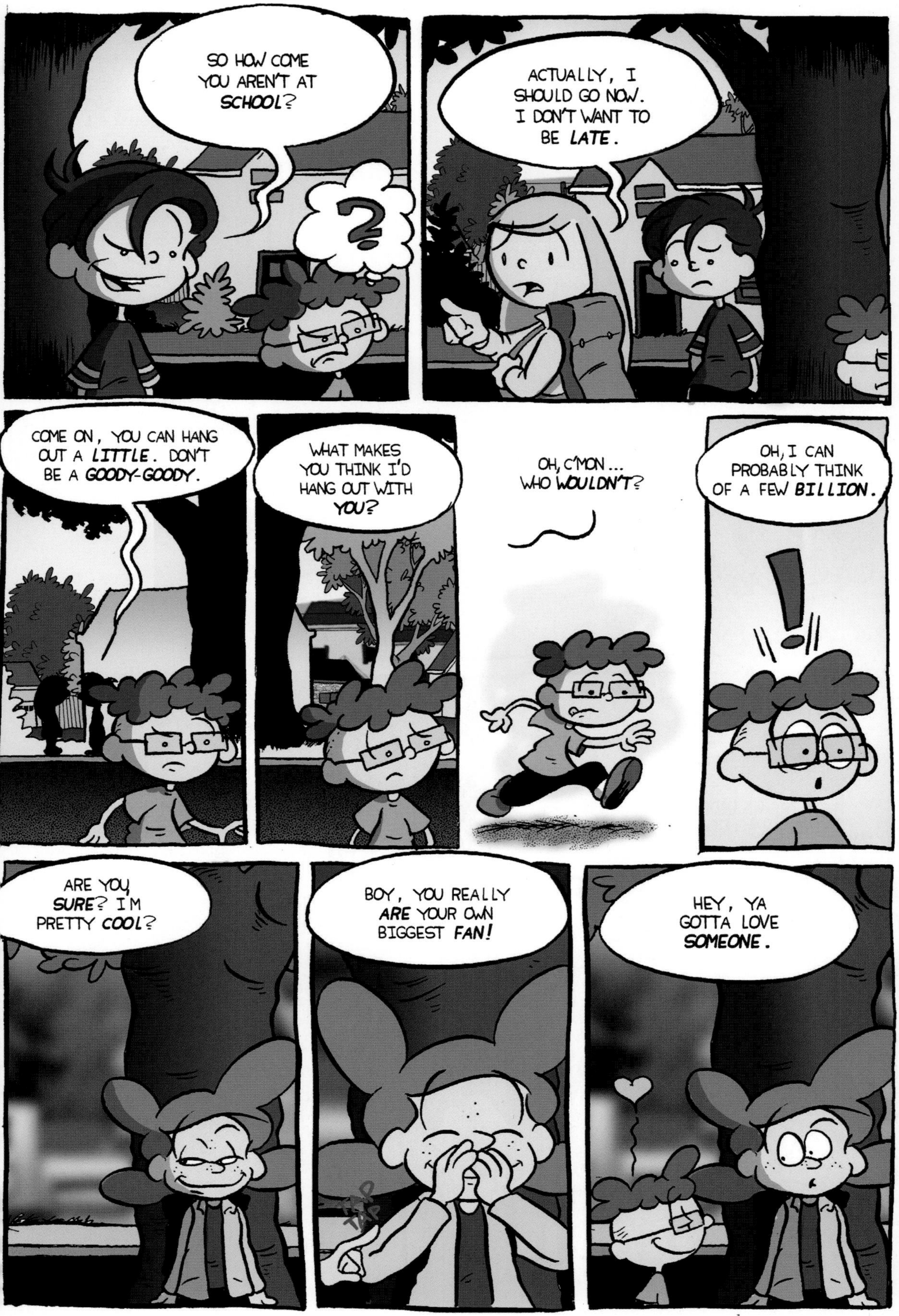
SO HOW COME YOU AREN'T AT SCHOOL?
?
ACTUALLY, I SHOULD GO NOW. I DON'T WANT TO BE LATE.
COME ON, YOU CAN HANG OUT A LITTLE. DON'T BE A GOODY-GOODY.
WHAT MAKES YOU THINK I'D HANG OUT WITH YOU?
OH, C'MON... WHO WOULDN'T?
OH, I CAN PROBABLY THINK OF A FEW BILLION.
!
ARE YOU SURE? I'M PRETTY COOL?
BOY, YOU REALLY ARE YOUR OWN BIGGEST FAN!
TAP TAP
HEY, YA GOTTA LOVE SOMEONE.

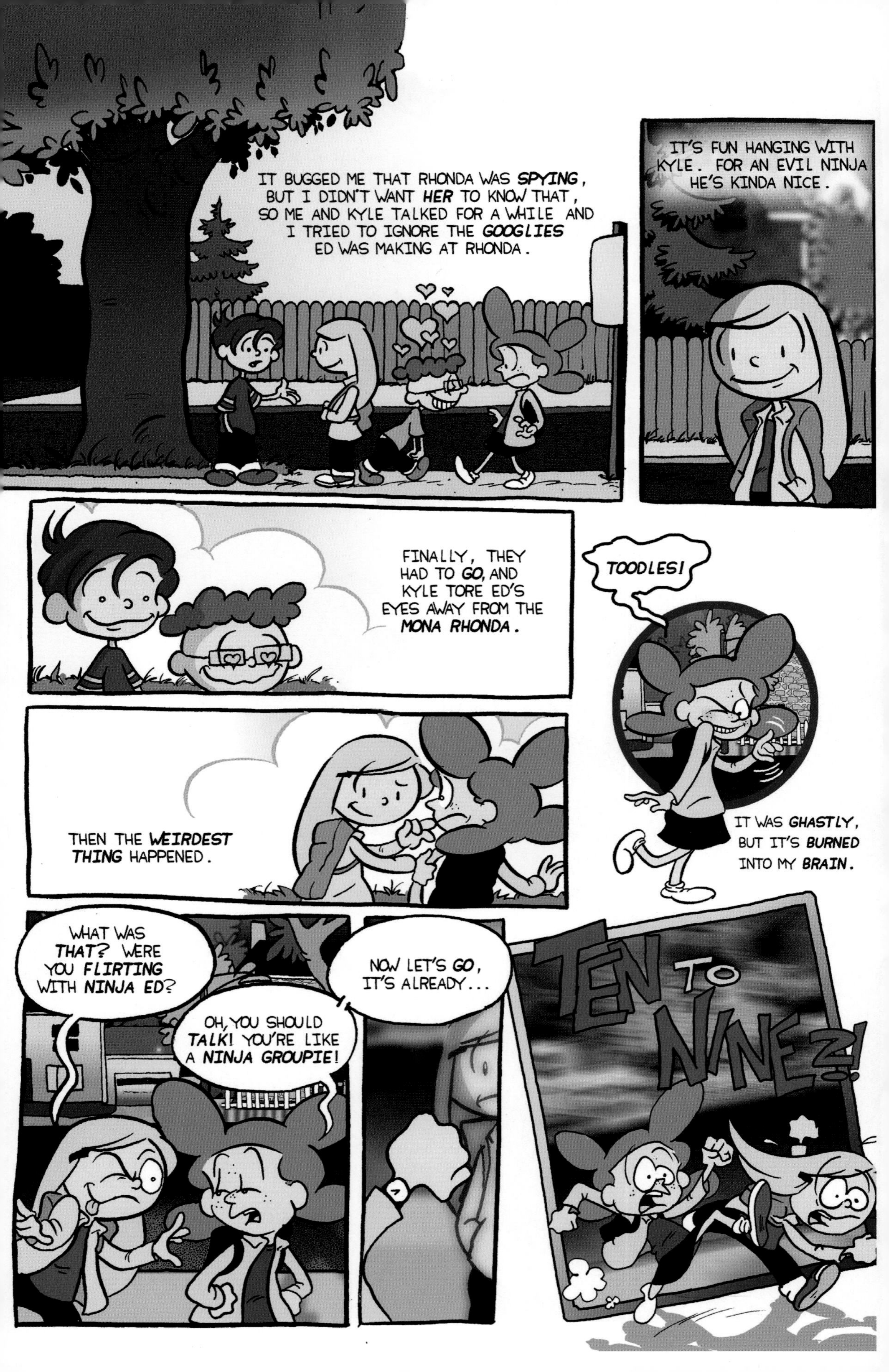
IT BUGGED ME THAT RHONDA WAS SPYING, BUT I DIDN'T WANT HER TO KNOW THAT, SO ME AND KYLE TALKED FOR A WHILE AND I TRIED TO IGNORE THE GOOGLIES ED WAS MAKING AT RHONDA.
IT'S FUN HANGING WITH KYLE. FOR AN EVIL NINJA HE'S KINDA NICE.
FINALLY, THEY HAD TO GO, AND KYLE TORE ED'S EYES AWAY FROM THE MONA RHONDA.
TOODLES!
THEN THE WEIRDEST THING HAPPENED.
IT WAS GHASTLY, BUT IT'S BURNED INTO MY BRAIN.
WHAT WAS THAT? WERE YOU FLIRTING WITH NINJA ED?
OH, YOU SHOULD TALK! YOU'RE LIKE A NINJA GROUPIE!
NOW LET'S GO, IT'S ALREADY...
TEN TO NINEZ!

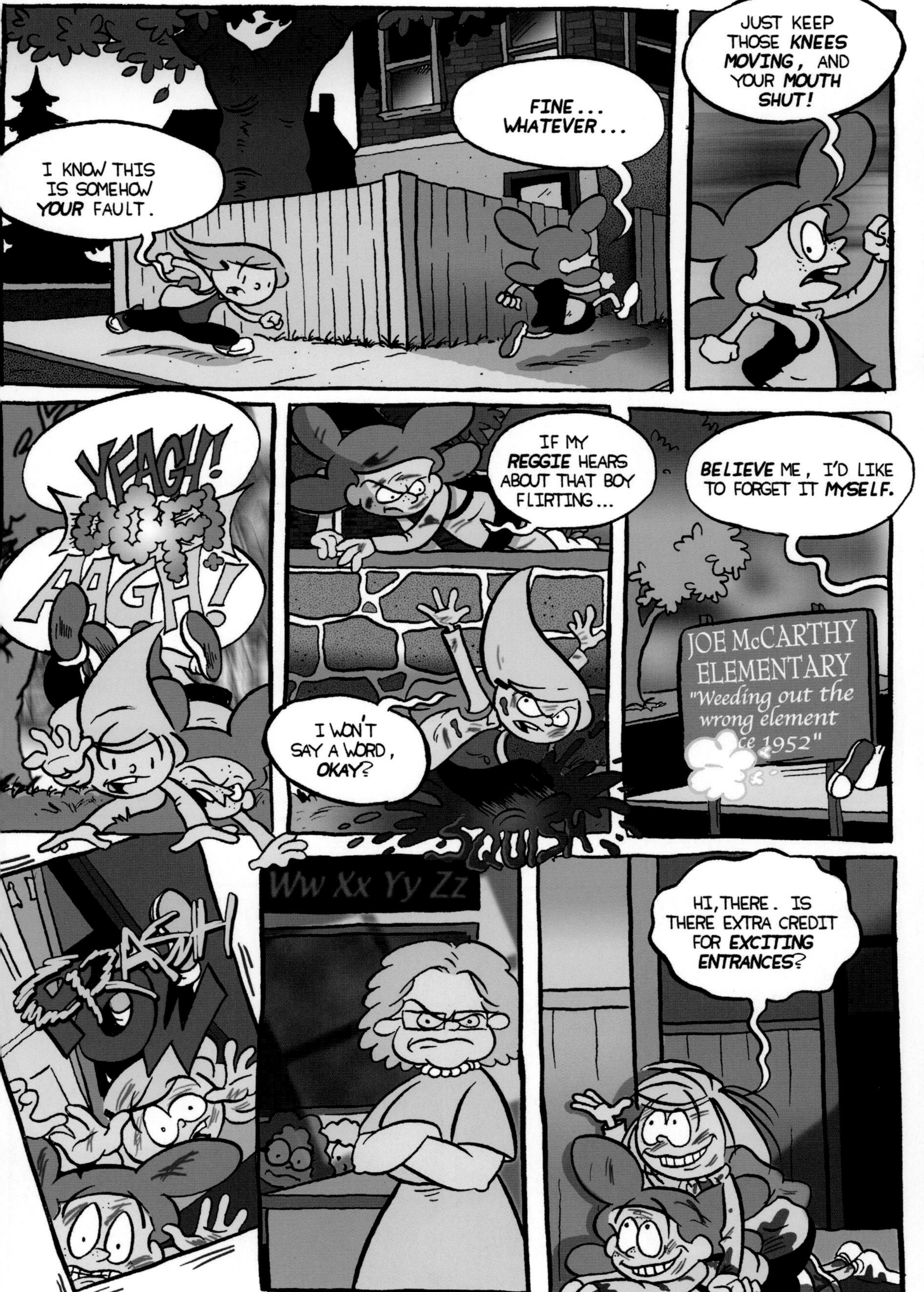
I KNOW THIS IS SOMEHOW YOUR FAULT.
FINE... WHATEVER...
JUST KEEP THOSE KNEES MOVING, AND YOUR MOUTH SHUT!
YEAGH! OOF! AAGH!
IF MY REGGIE HEARS ABOUT THAT BOY FLIRTING...
I WON'T SAY A WORD, OKAY?
BELIEVE ME, I'D LIKE TO FORGET IT MYSELF.
JOE McCARTHY ELEMENTARY
"Weeding out the wrong element ...ce 1952"
SQUISH
Ww Xx Yy Zz
HI, THERE. IS THERE EXTRA CREDIT FOR EXCITING ENTRANCES?

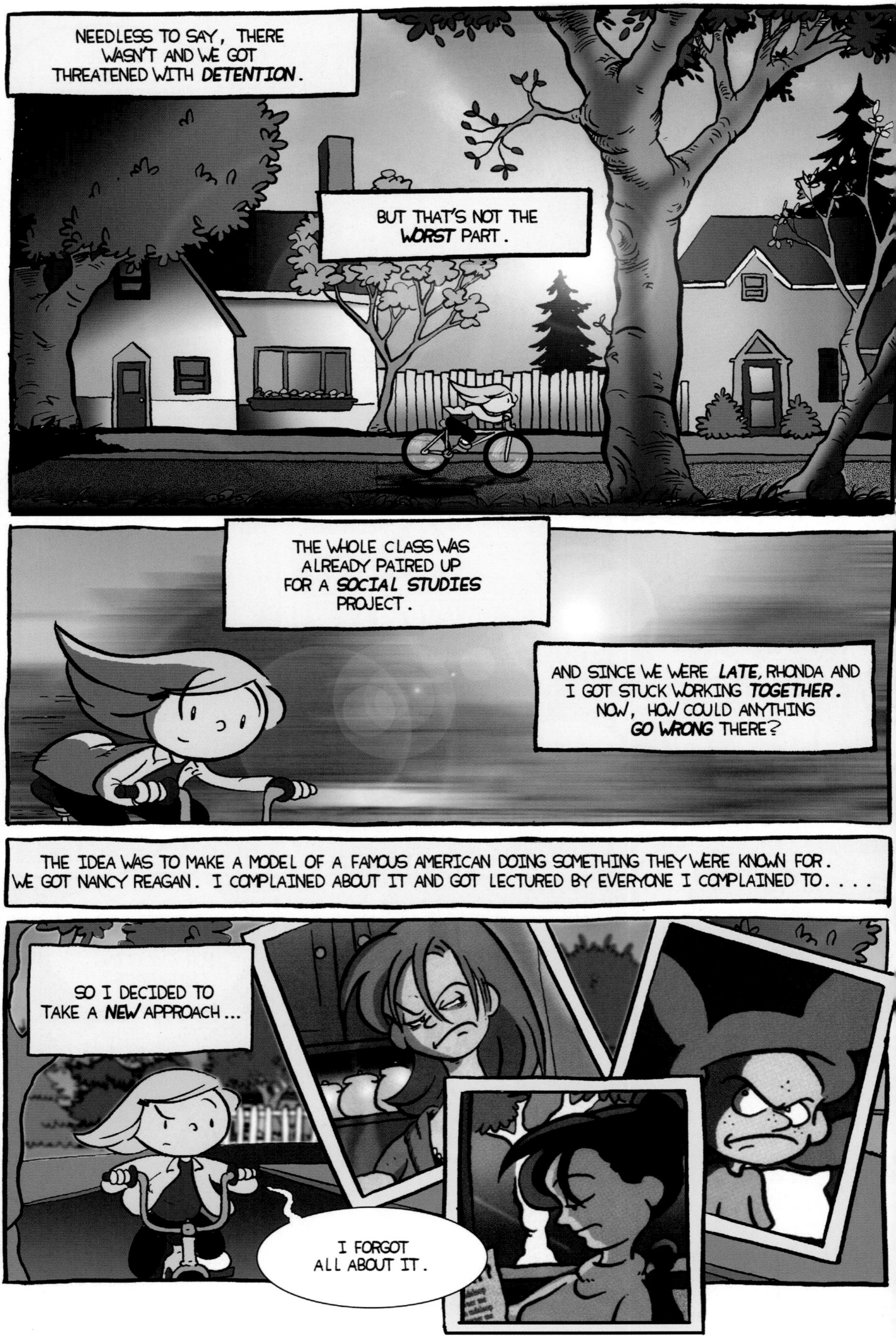
NEEDLESS TO SAY, THERE WASN'T AND WE GOT THREATENED WITH DETENTION.
BUT THAT'S NOT THE WORST PART.
THE WHOLE CLASS WAS ALREADY PAIRED UP FOR A SOCIAL STUDIES PROJECT.
AND SINCE WE WERE LATE, RHONDA AND I GOT STUCK WORKING TOGETHER. NOW, HOW COULD ANYTHING GO WRONG THERE?
THE IDEA WAS TO MAKE A MODEL OF A FAMOUS AMERICAN DOING SOMETHING THEY WERE KNOWN FOR. WE GOT NANCY REAGAN. I COMPLAINED ABOUT IT AND GOT LECTURED BY EVERYONE I COMPLAINED TO. . . .
SO I DECIDED TO TAKE A NEW APPROACH...
I FORGOT ALL ABOUT IT.

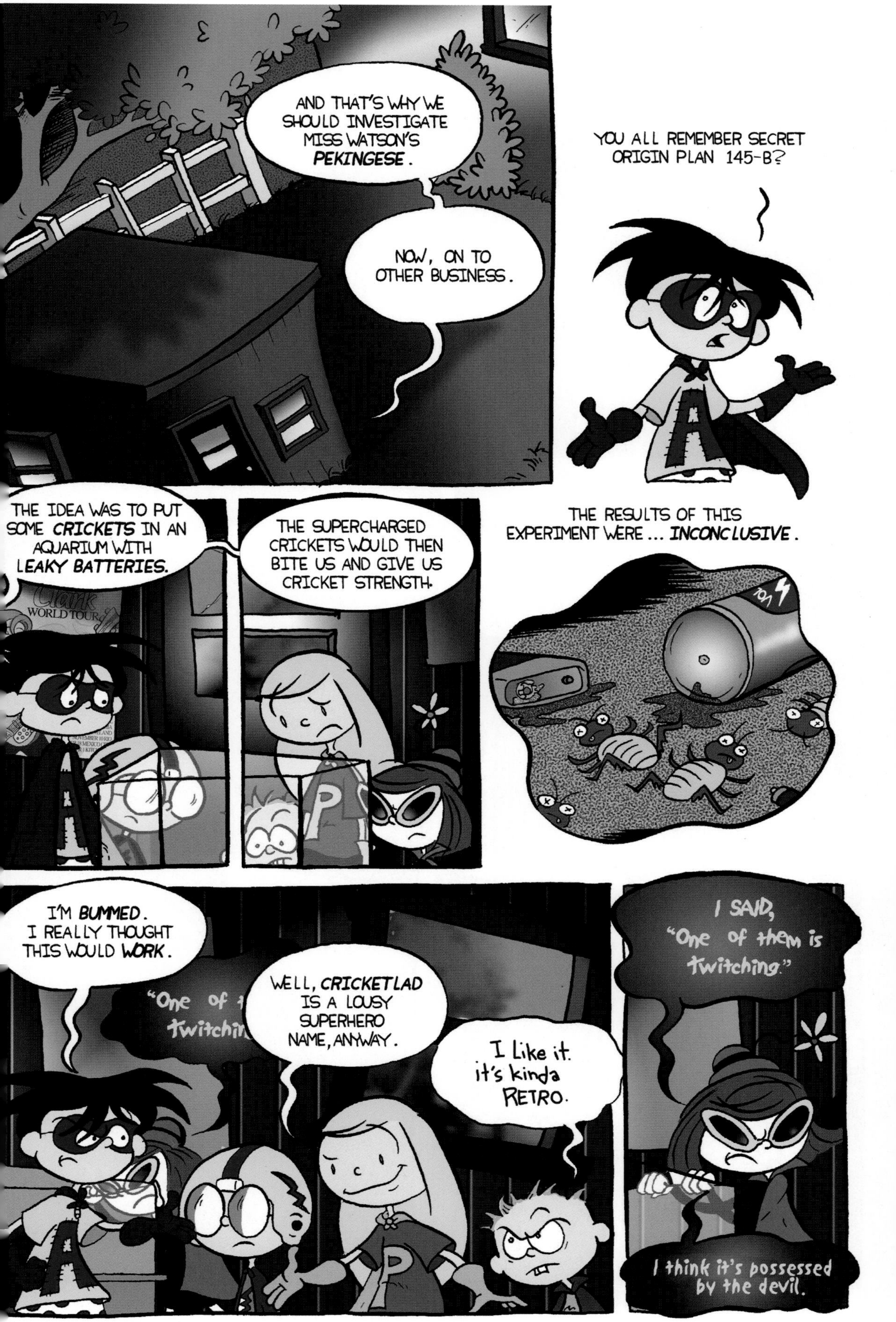
AND THAT'S WHY WE SHOULD INVESTIGATE MISS WATSON'S PEKINGESE.
NOW, ON TO OTHER BUSINESS.
YOU ALL REMEMBER SECRET ORIGIN PLAN 145-B?
THE IDEA WAS TO PUT SOME CRICKETS IN AN AQUARIUM WITH LEAKY BATTERIES.
THE SUPERCHARGED CRICKETS WOULD THEN BITE US AND GIVE US CRICKET STRENGTH.
THE RESULTS OF THIS EXPERIMENT WERE ... INCONCLUSIVE.
I'M BUMMED. I REALLY THOUGHT THIS WOULD WORK.
"One of t
twitchin
WELL, CRICKETLAD IS A LOUSY SUPERHERO NAME, ANYWAY.
I Like it. it's kinda RETRO.
I SAID, "One of them is twitching."
I think it's possessed by the devil.

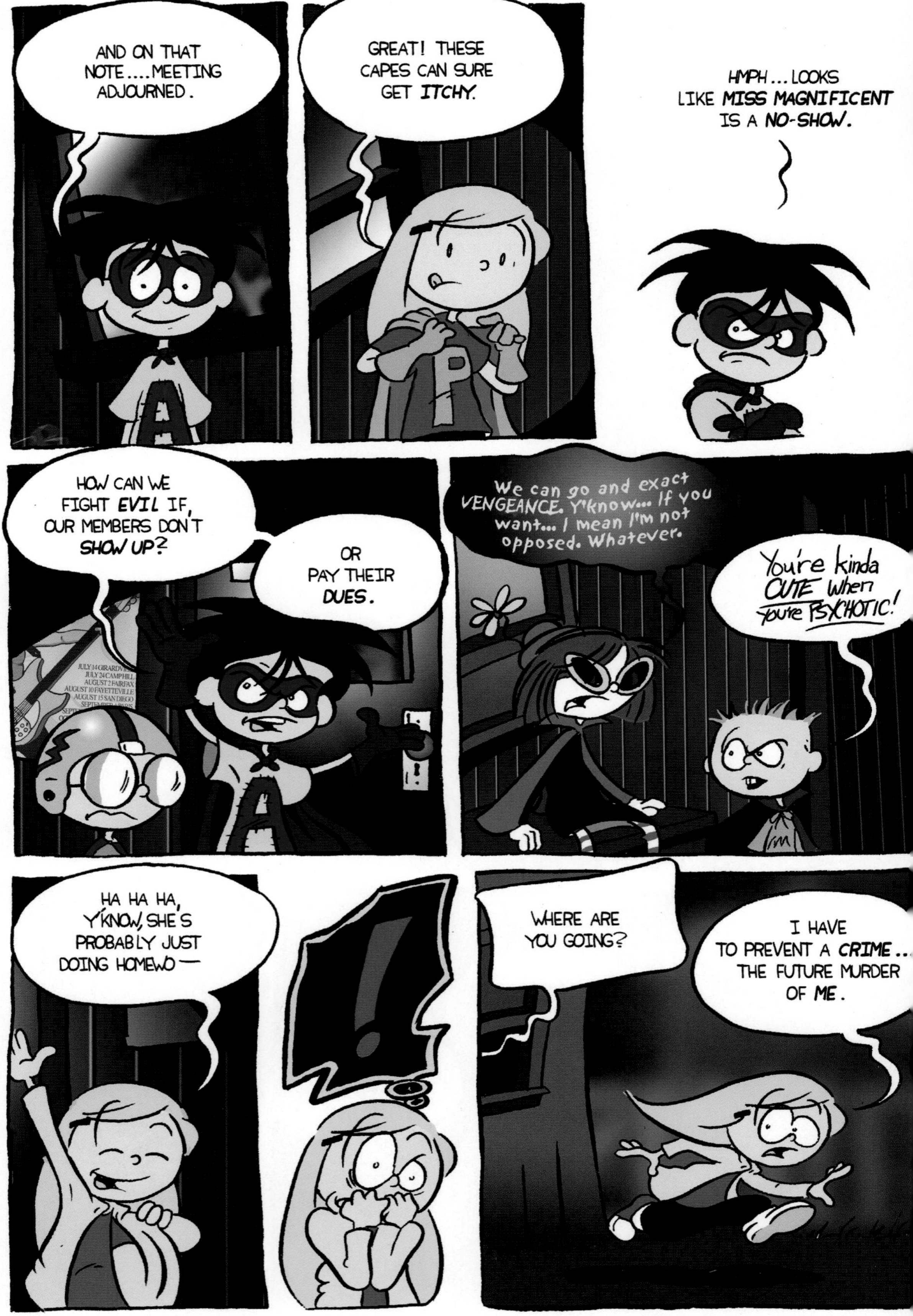

AND ON THAT NOTE....MEETING ADJOURNED.
GREAT! THESE CAPES CAN SURE GET ITCHY.
HMPH... LOOKS LIKE MISS MAGNIFICENT IS A NO-SHOW.
HOW CAN WE FIGHT EVIL IF, OUR MEMBERS DON'T SHOW UP?
OR PAY THEIR DUES.
We can go and exact VENGEANCE. Y'know... If you want... I mean I'm not opposed. Whatever.
You're kinda CUTE when you're PSYCHOTIC!
HA HA HA, Y'KNOW, SHE'S PROBABLY JUST DOING HOMEWO—
!
WHERE ARE YOU GOING?
I HAVE TO PREVENT A CRIME... THE FUTURE MURDER OF ME.

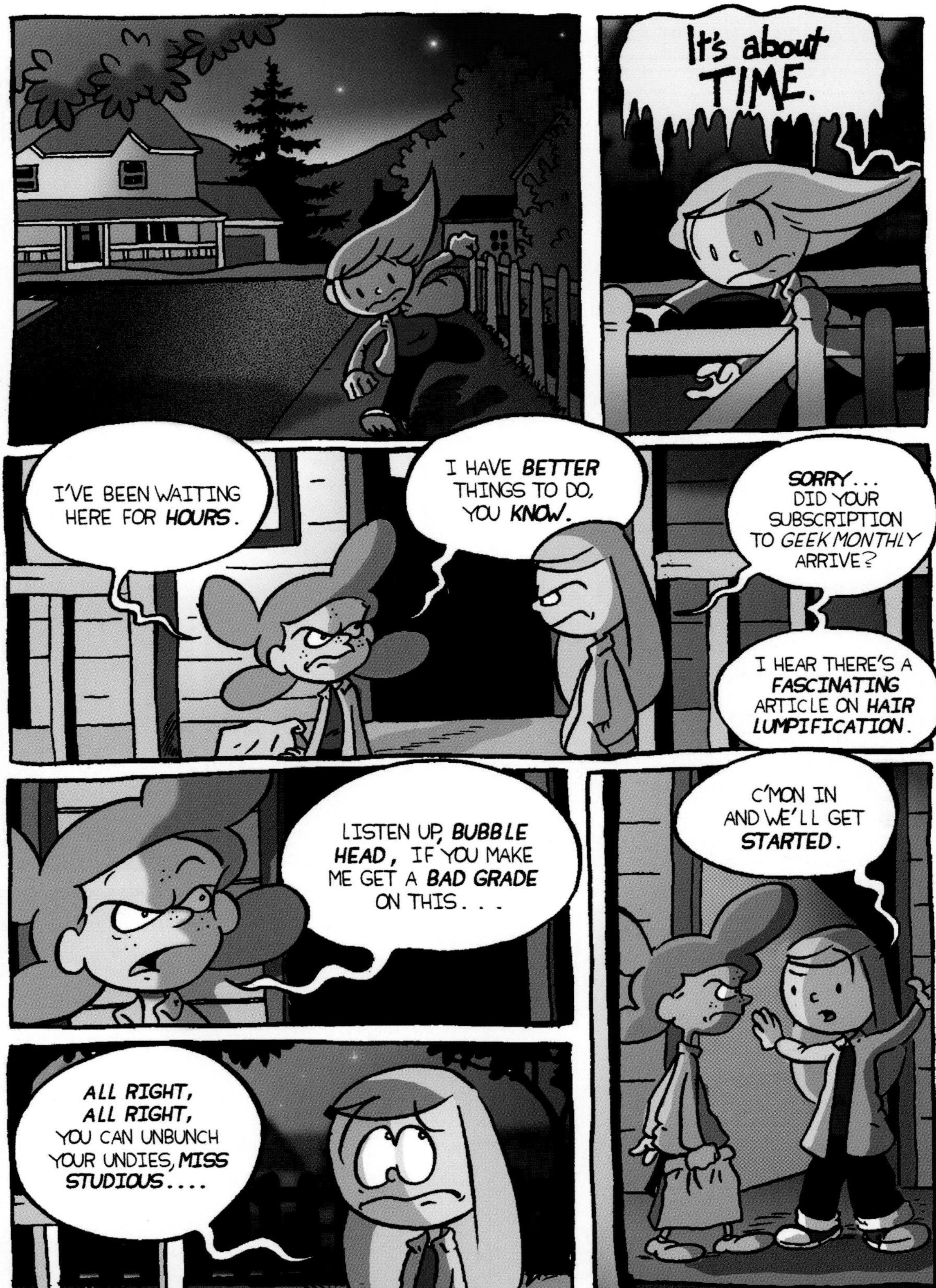
It's about TIME.
I'VE BEEN WAITING HERE FOR HOURS.
I HAVE BETTER THINGS TO DO, YOU KNOW.
SORRY... DID YOUR SUBSCRIPTION TO GEEK MONTHLY ARRIVE?
I HEAR THERE'S A FASCINATING ARTICLE ON HAIR LUMPIFICATION.
LISTEN UP, BUBBLE HEAD, IF YOU MAKE ME GET A BAD GRADE ON THIS. . .
ALL RIGHT, ALL RIGHT, YOU CAN UNBUNCH YOUR UNDIES, MISS STUDIOUS....
C'MON IN AND WE'LL GET STARTED.

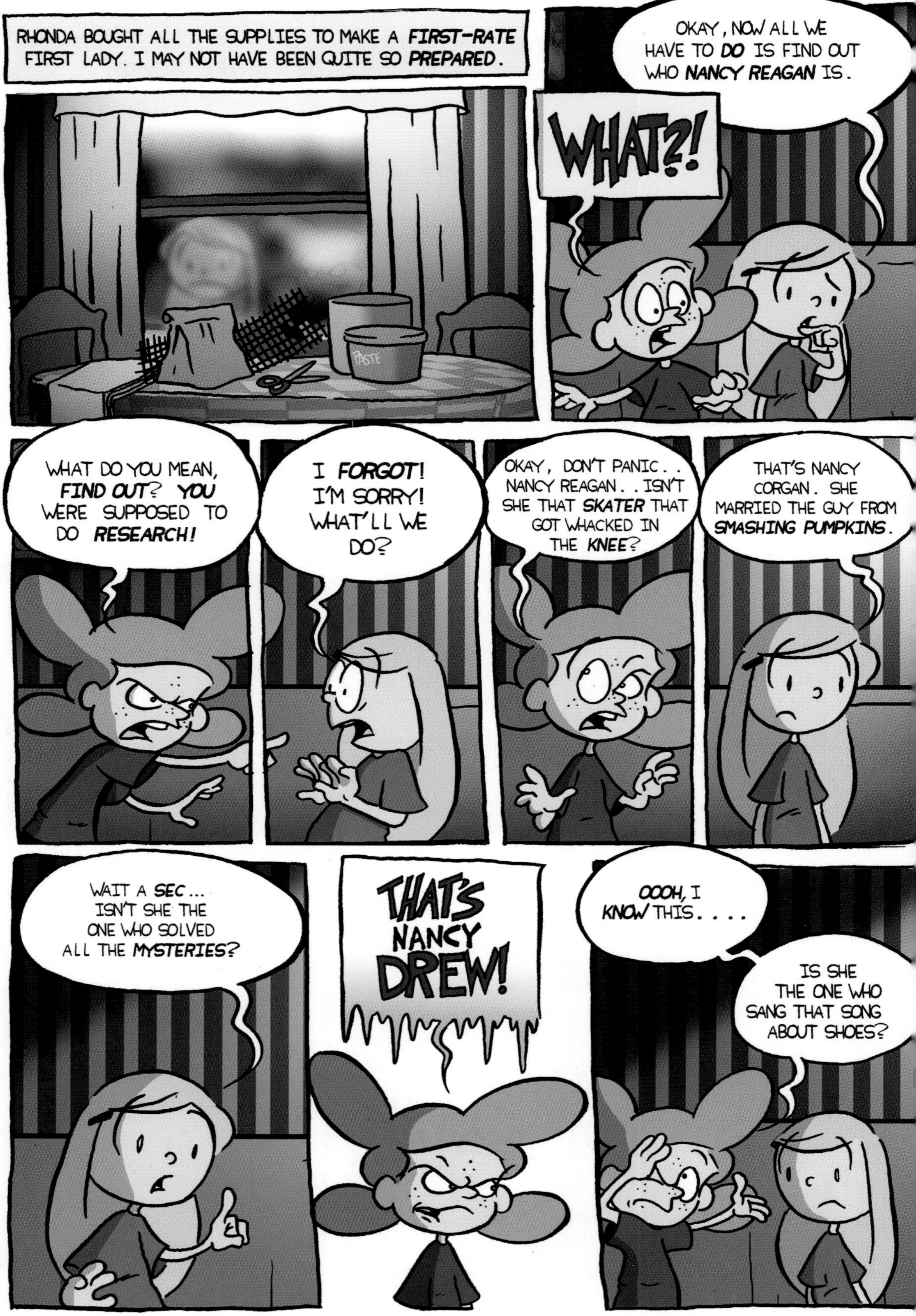
RHONDA BOUGHT ALL THE SUPPLIES TO MAKE A FIRST-RATE FIRST LADY. I MAY NOT HAVE BEEN QUITE SO PREPARED.
PASTE
OKAY, NOW ALL WE HAVE TO DO IS FIND OUT WHO NANCY REAGAN IS.
WHAT?!
WHAT DO YOU MEAN, FIND OUT? YOU WERE SUPPOSED TO DO RESEARCH!
I FORGOT! I'M SORRY! WHAT'LL WE DO?
OKAY, DON'T PANIC.. NANCY REAGAN..ISN'T SHE THAT SKATER THAT GOT WHACKED IN THE KNEE?
THAT'S NANCY CORGAN. SHE MARRIED THE GUY FROM SMASHING PUMPKINS.
WAIT A SEC... ISN'T SHE THE ONE WHO SOLVED ALL THE MYSTERIES?
THAT'S NANCY DREW!
OOOH, I KNOW THIS....
IS SHE THE ONE WHO SANG THAT SONG ABOUT SHOES?

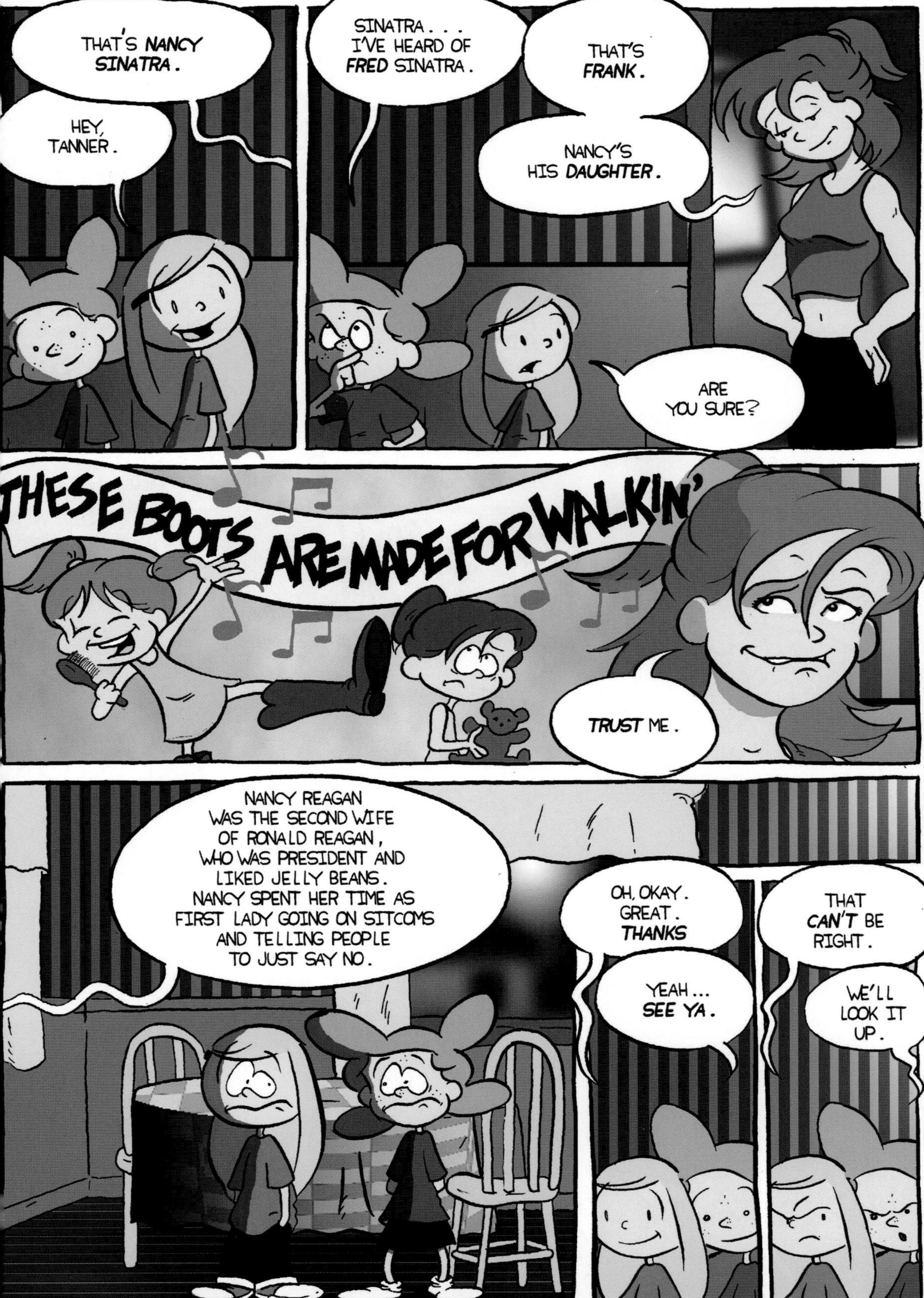
THAT'S NANCY SINATRA.
HEY, TANNER.
SINATRA... I'VE HEARD OF FRED SINATRA.
THAT'S FRANK.
NANCY'S HIS DAUGHTER.
ARE YOU SURE?
THESE BOOTS ARE MADE FOR WALKIN'
TRUST ME.
NANCY REAGAN WAS THE SECOND WIFE OF RONALD REAGAN, WHO WAS PRESIDENT AND LIKED JELLY BEANS. NANCY SPENT HER TIME AS FIRST LADY GOING ON SITCOMS AND TELLING PEOPLE TO JUST SAY NO.
OH, OKAY. GREAT. THANKS
YEAH... SEE YA.
THAT CAN'T BE RIGHT.
WE'LL LOOK IT UP.

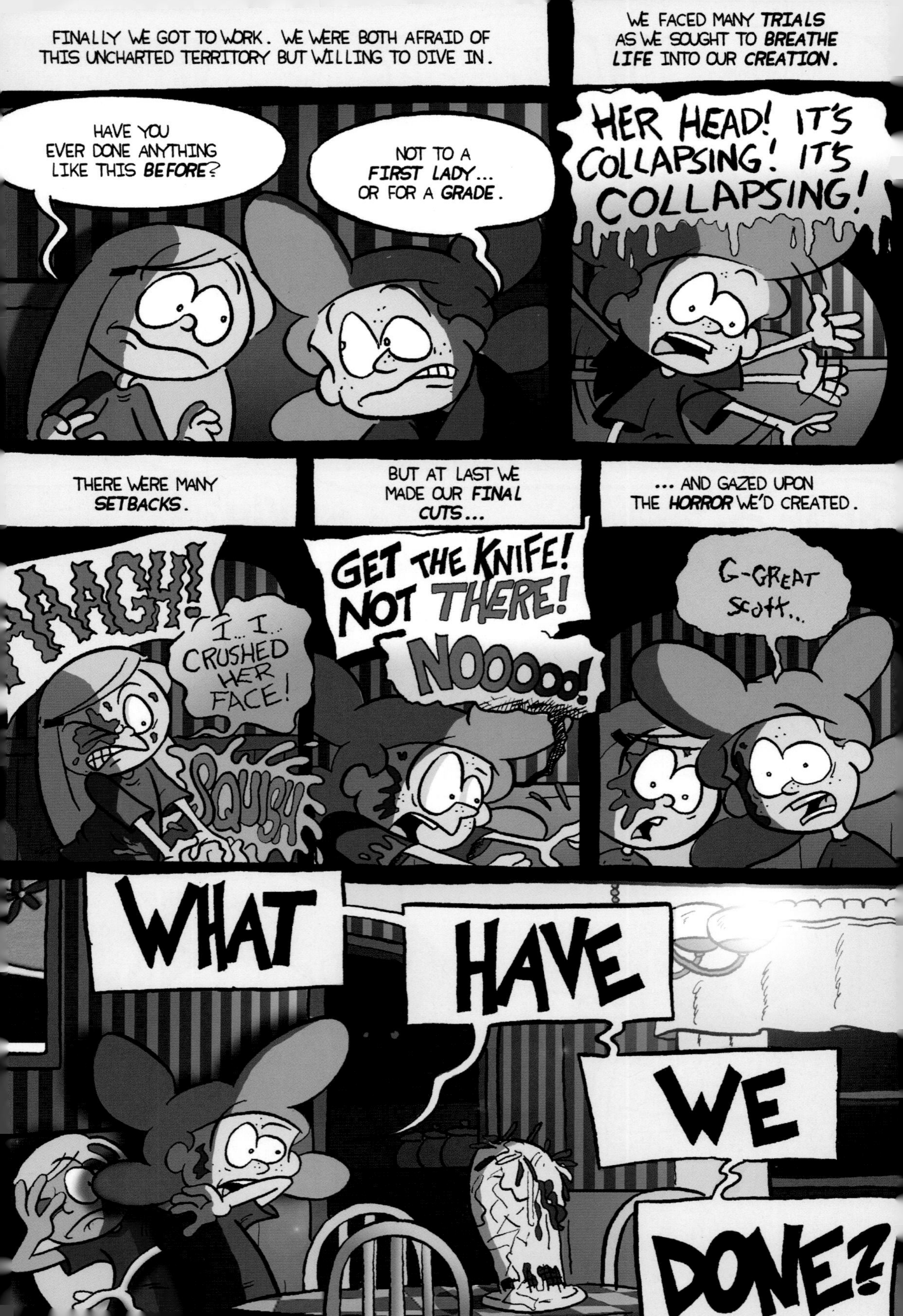
FINALLY WE GOT TO WORK. WE WERE BOTH AFRAID OF THIS UNCHARTED TERRITORY BUT WILLING TO DIVE IN.
HAVE YOU EVER DONE ANYTHING LIKE THIS BEFORE?
NOT TO A FIRST LADY... OR FOR A GRADE.
WE FACED MANY TRIALS AS WE SOUGHT TO BREATHE LIFE INTO OUR CREATION.
HER HEAD! IT'S COLLAPSING! IT'S COLLAPSING!
THERE WERE MANY SETBACKS.
AAGH!
I.. I.. CRUSHED HER FACE!
SQUISH
BUT AT LAST WE MADE OUR FINAL CUTS...
GET THE KNIFE! NOT THERE!
NOOOOOO!
... AND GAZED UPON THE HORROR WE'D CREATED.
G-GREAT Scott...
WHAT
HAVE
WE
DONE?

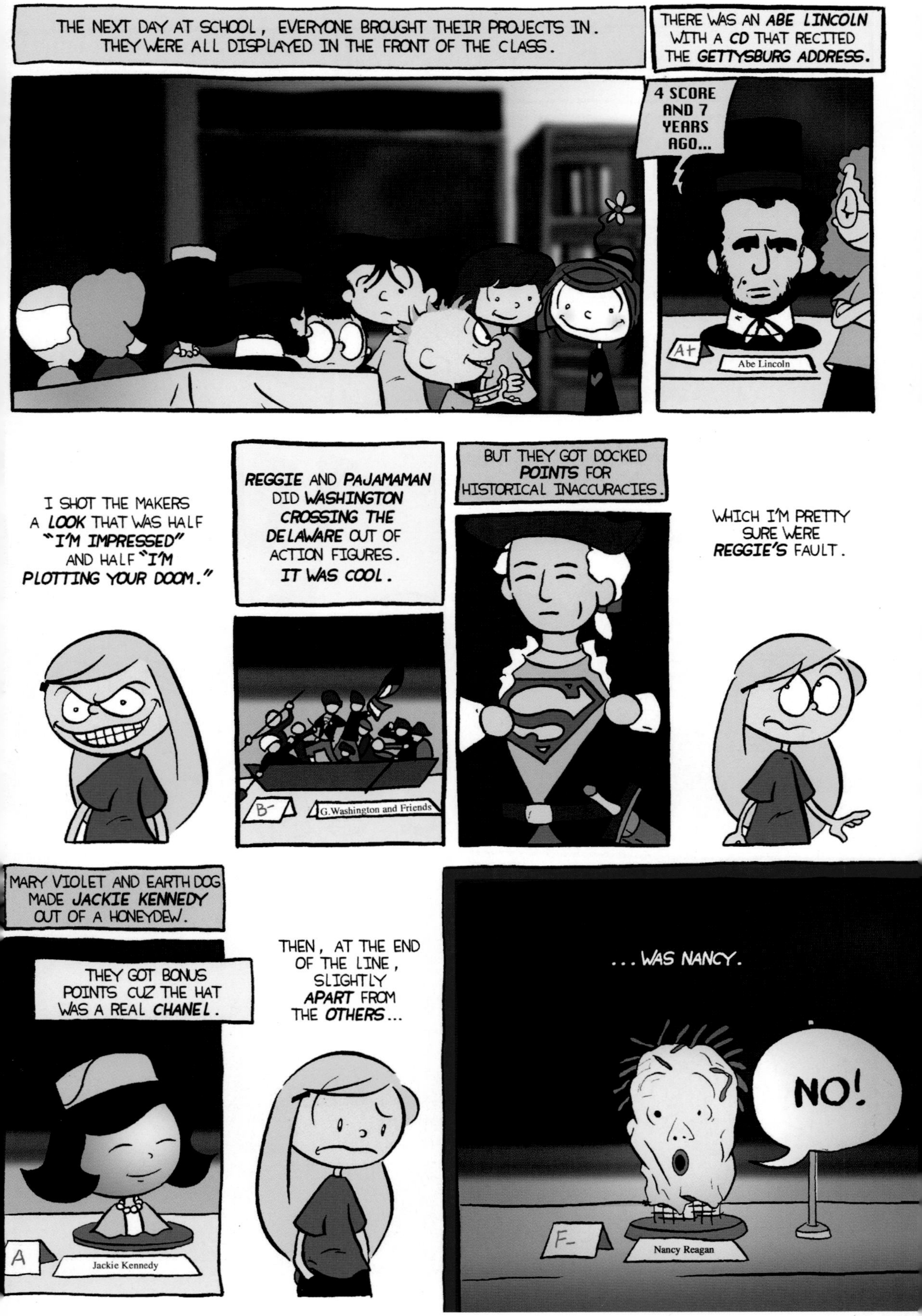
THE NEXT DAY AT SCHOOL, EVERYONE BROUGHT THEIR PROJECTS IN. THEY WERE ALL DISPLAYED IN THE FRONT OF THE CLASS.
THERE WAS AN ABE LINCOLN WITH A CD THAT RECITED THE GETTYSBURG ADDRESS.
4 SCORE AND 7 YEARS AGO...
A+
Abe Lincoln
I SHOT THE MAKERS A LOOK THAT WAS HALF "I'M IMPRESSED" AND HALF "I'M PLOTTING YOUR DOOM."
REGGIE AND PAJAMAMAN DID WASHINGTON CROSSING THE DELAWARE OUT OF ACTION FIGURES. IT WAS COOL.
B-
G.Washington and Friends
BUT THEY GOT DOCKED POINTS FOR HISTORICAL INACCURACIES.
WHICH I'M PRETTY SURE WERE REGGIE'S FAULT.
MARY VIOLET AND EARTH DOG MADE JACKIE KENNEDY OUT OF A HONEYDEW.
THEY GOT BONUS POINTS CUZ THE HAT WAS A REAL CHANEL.
A
Jackie Kennedy
THEN, AT THE END OF THE LINE, SLIGHTLY APART FROM THE OTHERS...
...WAS NANCY.
NO!
F-
Nancy Reagan

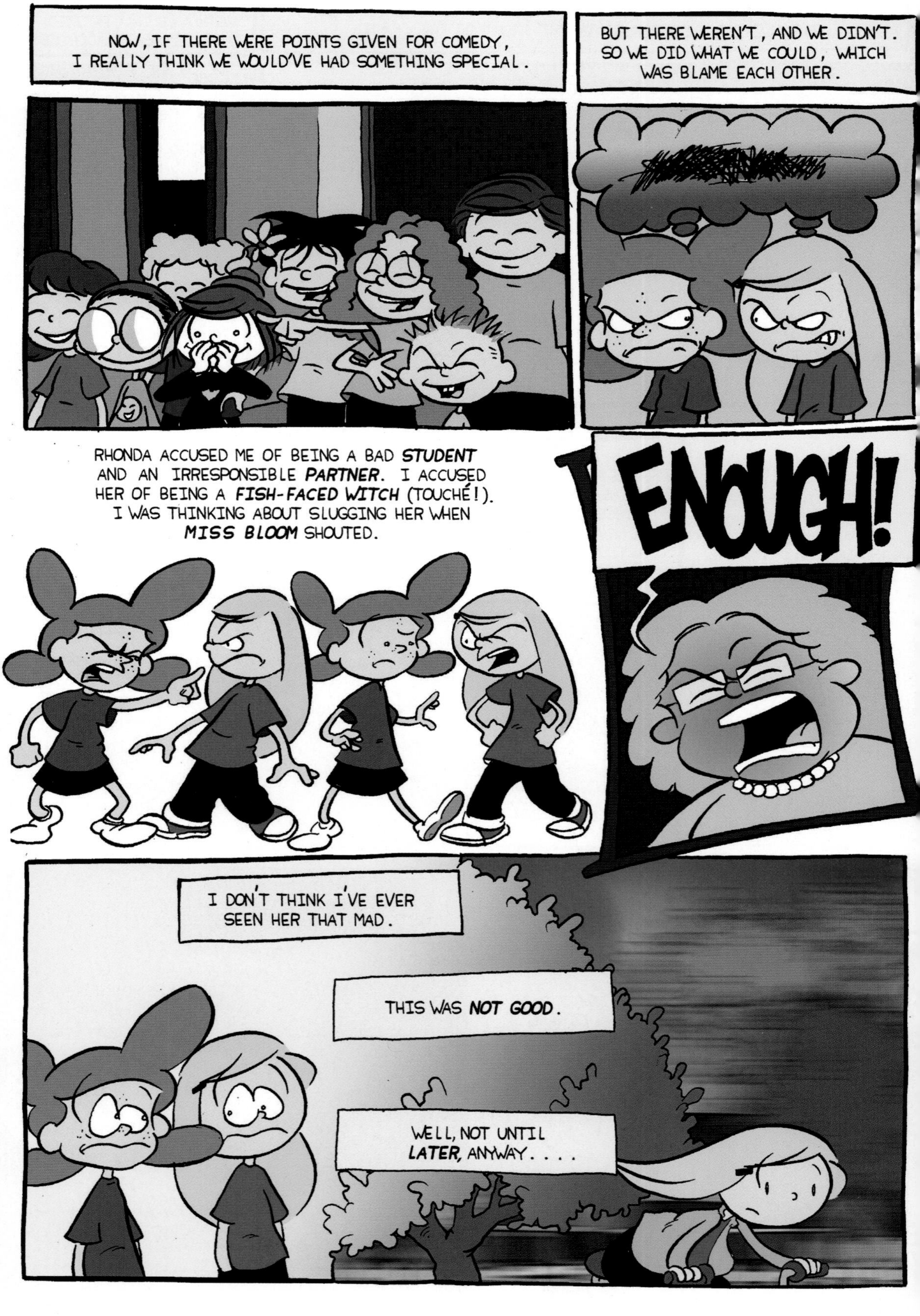
NOW, IF THERE WERE POINTS GIVEN FOR COMEDY, I REALLY THINK WE WOULD'VE HAD SOMETHING SPECIAL.
BUT THERE WEREN'T, AND WE DIDN'T. SO WE DID WHAT WE COULD, WHICH WAS BLAME EACH OTHER.
RHONDA ACCUSED ME OF BEING A BAD STUDENT AND AN IRRESPONSIBLE PARTNER. I ACCUSED HER OF BEING A FISH-FACED WITCH (TOUCHÉ!). I WAS THINKING ABOUT SLUGGING HER WHEN MISS BLOOM SHOUTED.
ENOUGH!
I DON'T THINK I'VE EVER SEEN HER THAT MAD.
THIS WAS NOT GOOD.
WELL, NOT UNTIL LATER, ANYWAY. . . .

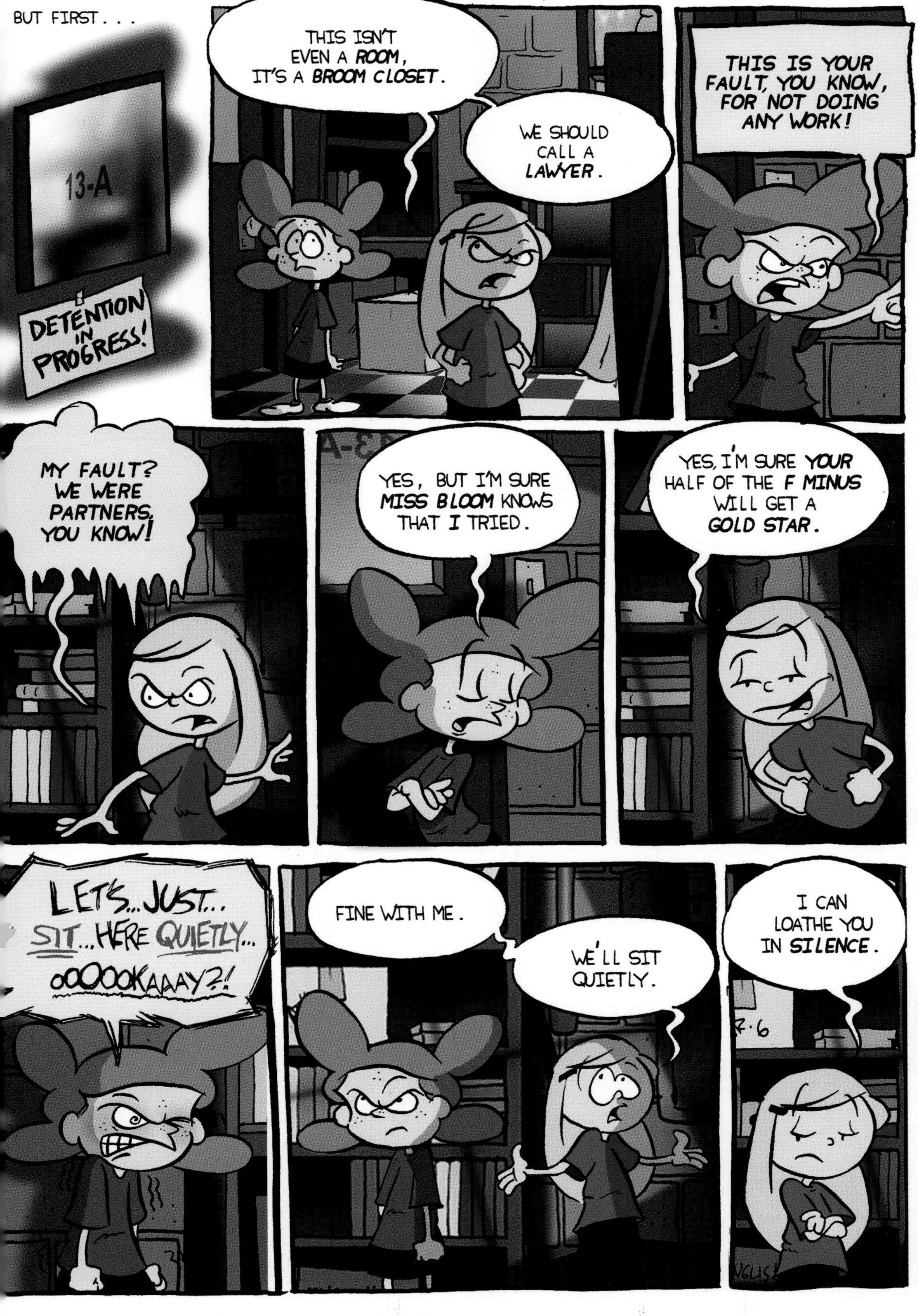
BUT FIRST . . .
13-A
DETENTION IN PROGRESS!
THIS ISN'T EVEN A ROOM, IT'S A BROOM CLOSET.
WE SHOULD CALL A LAWYER.
THIS IS YOUR FAULT, YOU KNOW, FOR NOT DOING ANY WORK!
MY FAULT? WE WERE PARTNERS, YOU KNOW!
YES, BUT I'M SURE MISS BLOOM KNOWS THAT I TRIED.
YES, I'M SURE YOUR HALF OF THE F MINUS WILL GET A GOLD STAR.
LET'S...JUST... SIT...HERE QUIETLY... oOOOOKAAAY?!
FINE WITH ME.
WE'LL SIT QUIETLY.
I CAN LOATHE YOU IN SILENCE.

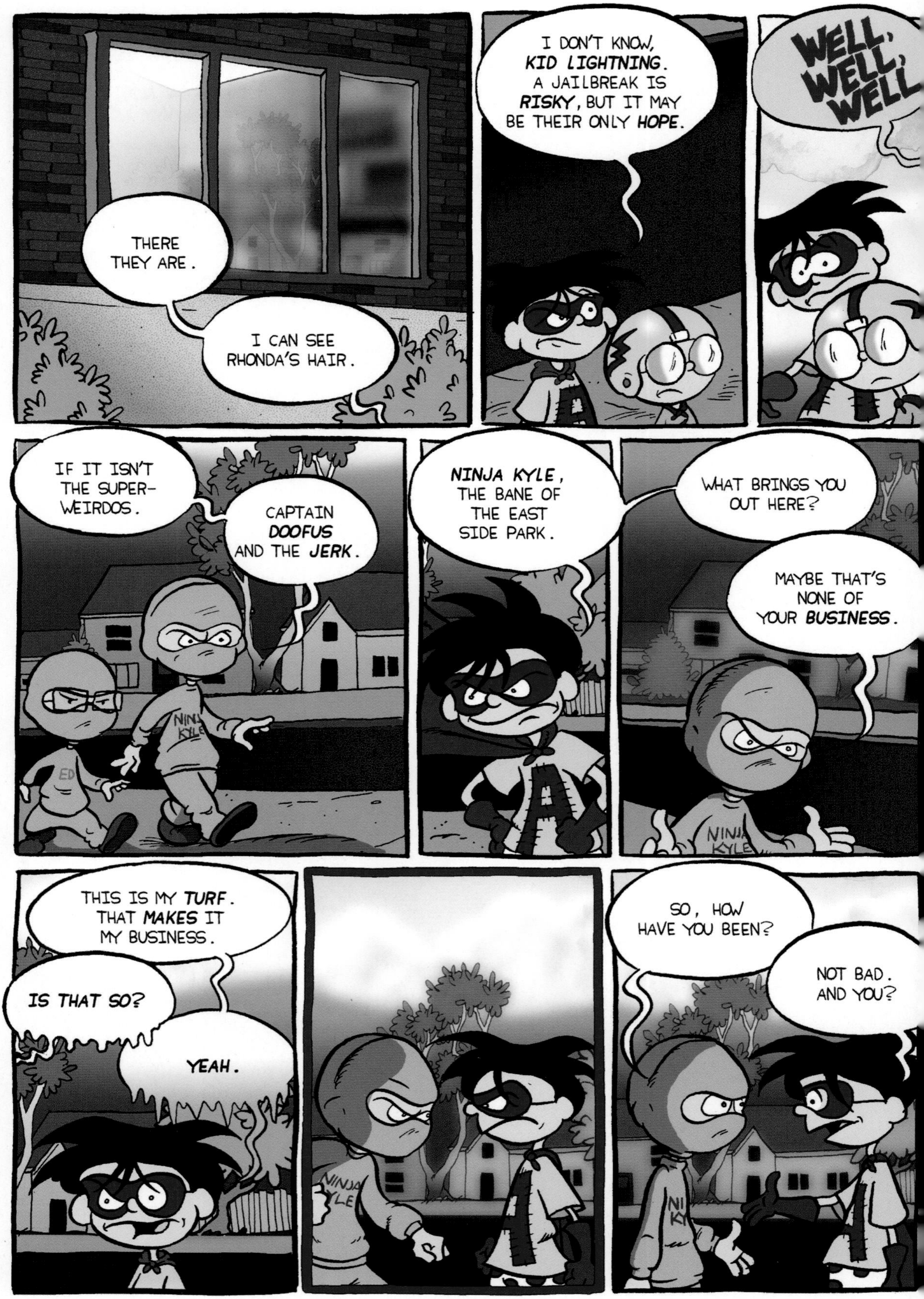
THERE THEY ARE.
I CAN SEE RHONDA'S HAIR.
I DON'T KNOW, KID LIGHTNING. A JAILBREAK IS RISKY, BUT IT MAY BE THEIR ONLY HOPE.
WELL, WELL, WELL
IF IT ISN'T THE SUPER-WEIRDOS.
CAPTAIN DOOFUS AND THE JERK.
NINJA KYLE
ED
NINJA KYLE, THE BANE OF THE EAST SIDE PARK.
WHAT BRINGS YOU OUT HERE?
MAYBE THAT'S NONE OF YOUR BUSINESS.
NINJA KYLE
THIS IS MY TURF. THAT MAKES IT MY BUSINESS.
IS THAT SO?
YEAH.
NINJA KYLE
SO, HOW HAVE YOU BEEN?
NOT BAD. AND YOU?

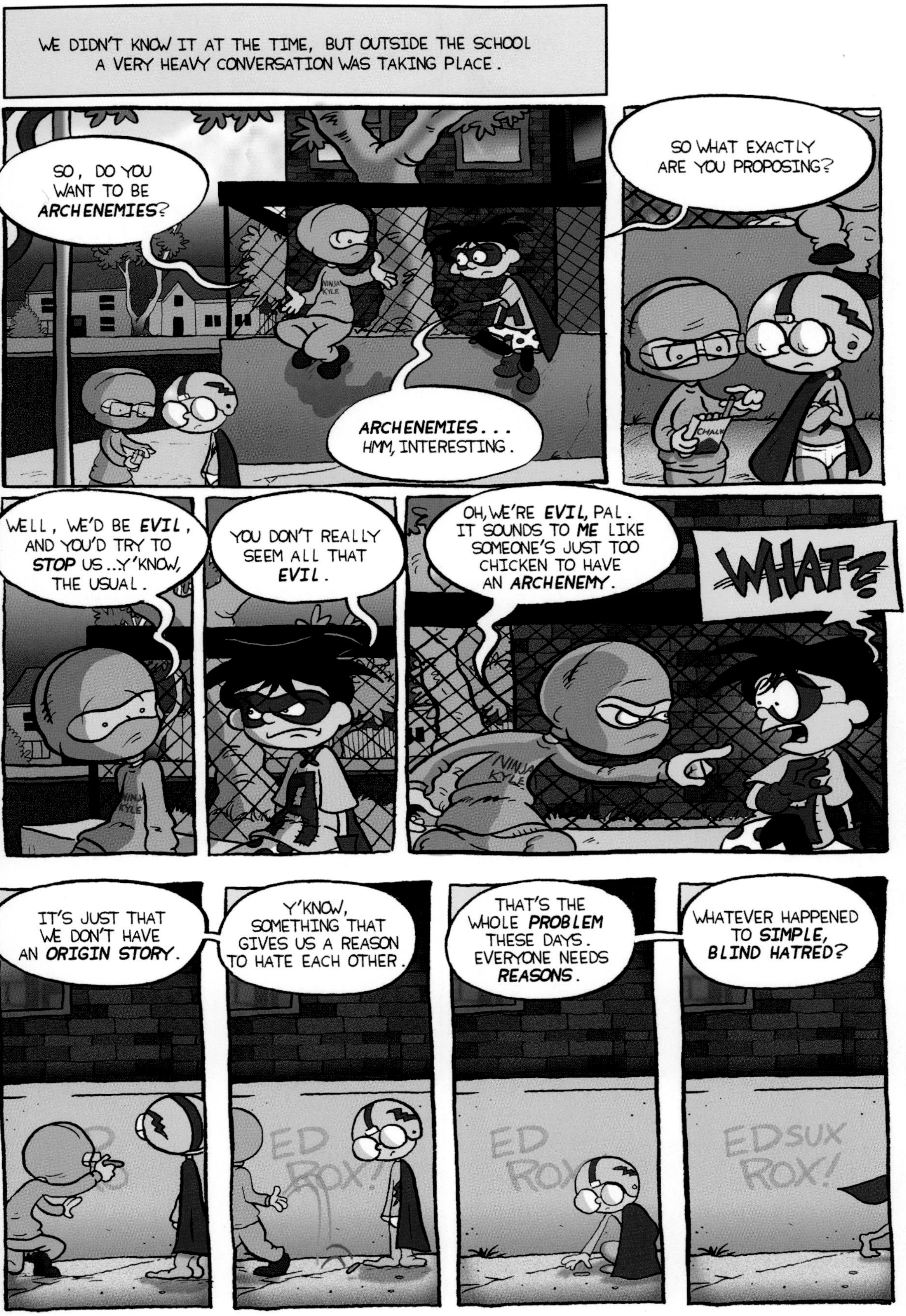
WE DIDN'T KNOW IT AT THE TIME, BUT OUTSIDE THE SCHOOL A VERY HEAVY CONVERSATION WAS TAKING PLACE.
SO, DO YOU WANT TO BE ARCHENEMIES?
NINJA KYLE
ARCHENEMIES... HMM, INTERESTING.
SO WHAT EXACTLY ARE YOU PROPOSING?
CHALK
WELL, WE'D BE EVIL, AND YOU'D TRY TO STOP US...Y'KNOW, THE USUAL.
NINJA KYLE
YOU DON'T REALLY SEEM ALL THAT EVIL.
OH, WE'RE EVIL, PAL. IT SOUNDS TO ME LIKE SOMEONE'S JUST TOO CHICKEN TO HAVE AN ARCHENEMY.
WHAT?
NINJA KYLE
IT'S JUST THAT WE DON'T HAVE AN ORIGIN STORY.
Y'KNOW, SOMETHING THAT GIVES US A REASON TO HATE EACH OTHER.
ED ROX!
THAT'S THE WHOLE PROBLEM THESE DAYS. EVERYONE NEEDS REASONS.
ED ROX
WHATEVER HAPPENED TO SIMPLE, BLIND HATRED?
ED SUX ROX!

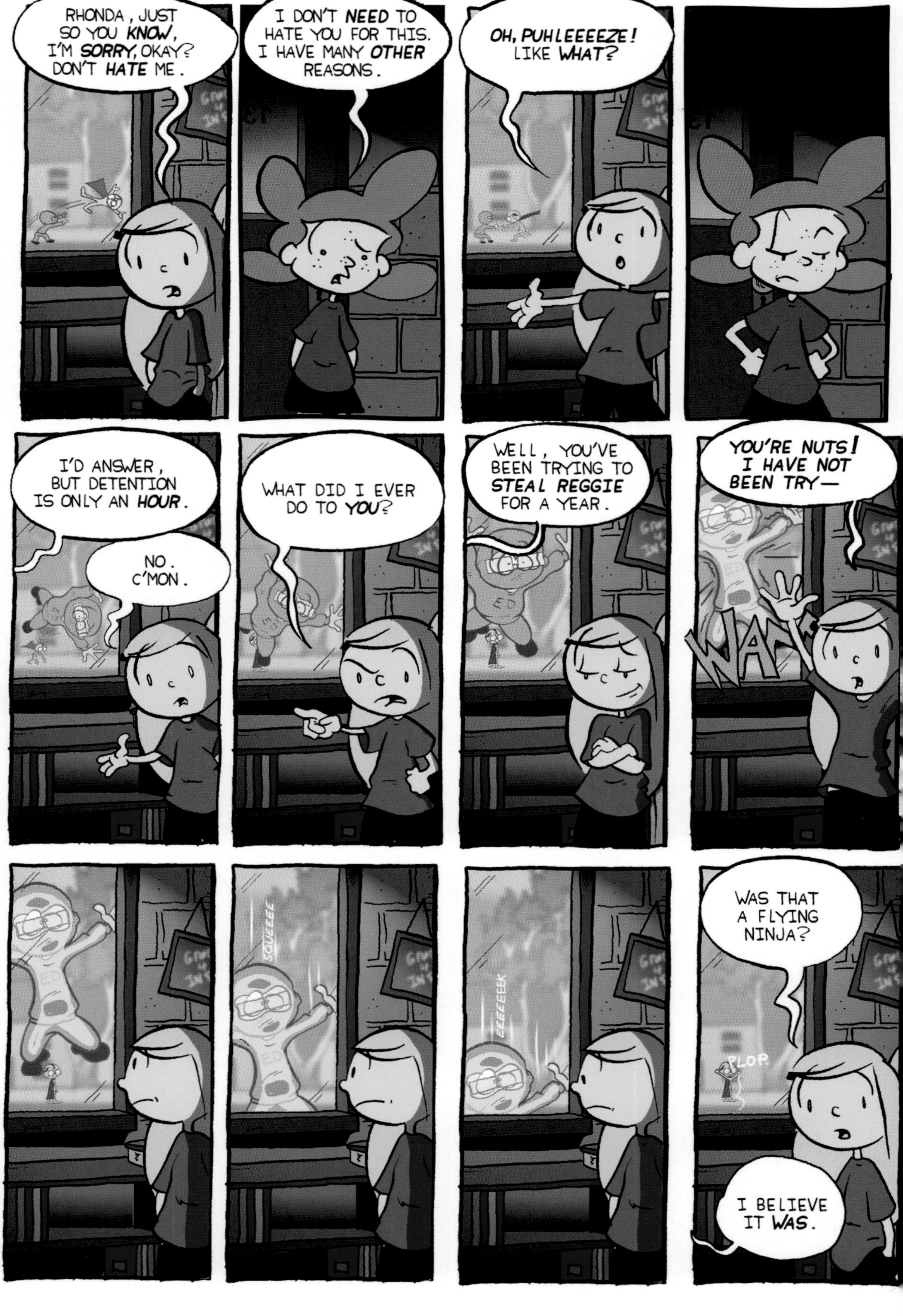
RHONDA, JUST SO YOU KNOW, I'M SORRY, OKAY? DON'T HATE ME.
I DON'T NEED TO HATE YOU FOR THIS. I HAVE MANY OTHER REASONS.
OH, PUHLEEEEZE! LIKE WHAT?
I'D ANSWER, BUT DETENTION IS ONLY AN HOUR.
NO. C'MON.
WHAT DID I EVER DO TO YOU?
WELL, YOU'VE BEEN TRYING TO STEAL REGGIE FOR A YEAR.
YOU'RE NUTS! I HAVE NOT BEEN TRY—
SQUEEEEE
EEEEEEEK
PLOP.
WAS THAT A FLYING NINJA?
I BELIEVE IT WAS.

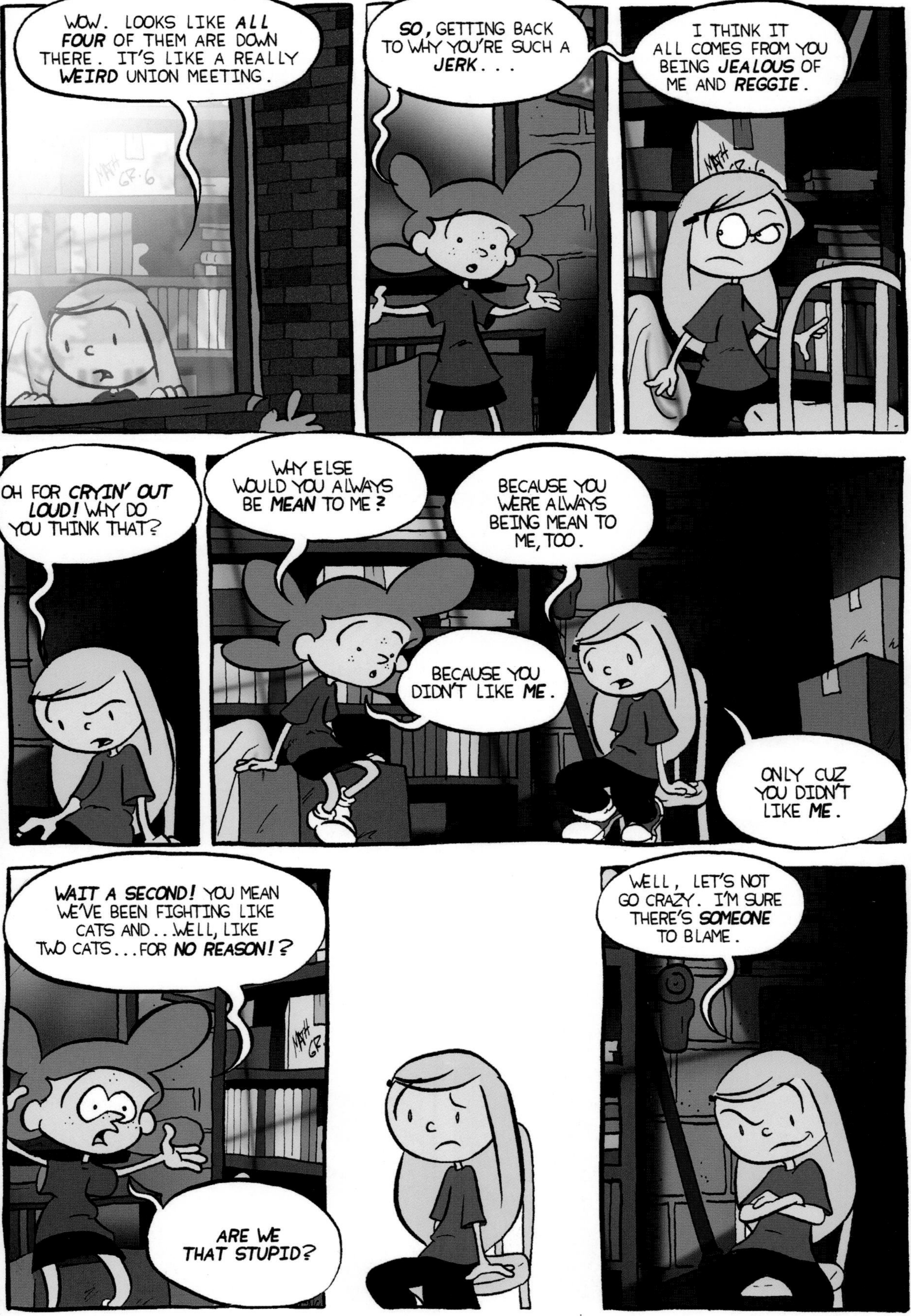
WOW. LOOKS LIKE ALL FOUR OF THEM ARE DOWN THERE. IT'S LIKE A REALLY WEIRD UNION MEETING.
MATH GR. 6
SO, GETTING BACK TO WHY YOU'RE SUCH A JERK...
I THINK IT ALL COMES FROM YOU BEING JEALOUS OF ME AND REGGIE.
OH FOR CRYIN' OUT LOUD! WHY DO YOU THINK THAT?
WHY ELSE WOULD YOU ALWAYS BE MEAN TO ME?
BECAUSE YOU WERE ALWAYS BEING MEAN TO ME, TOO.
BECAUSE YOU DIDN'T LIKE ME.
ONLY CUZ YOU DIDN'T LIKE ME.
WAIT A SECOND! YOU MEAN WE'VE BEEN FIGHTING LIKE CATS AND...WELL, LIKE TWO CATS...FOR NO REASON!?
ARE WE THAT STUPID?
WELL, LET'S NOT GO CRAZY. I'M SURE THERE'S SOMEONE TO BLAME.

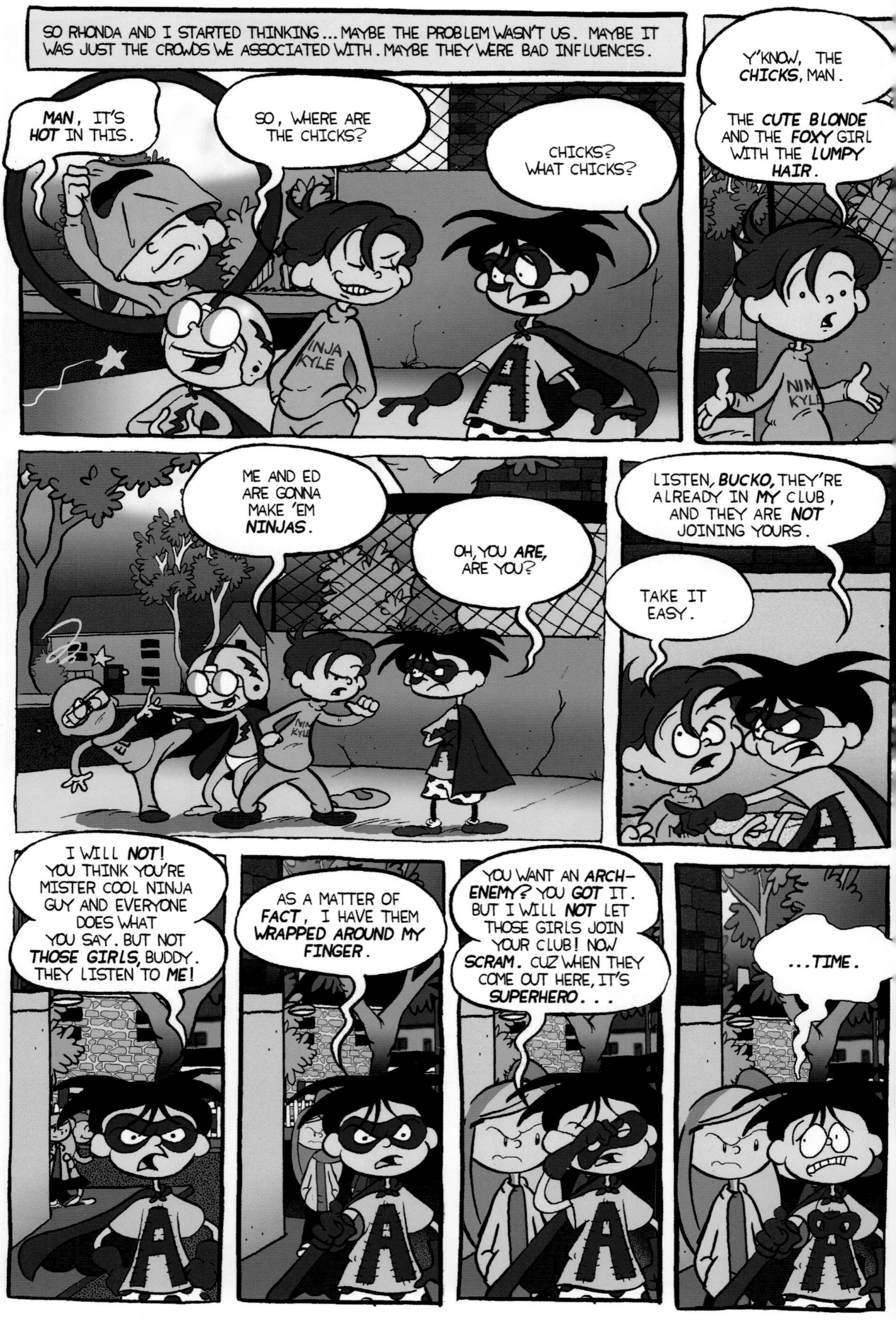
SO RHONDA AND I STARTED THINKING... MAYBE THE PROBLEM WASN'T US. MAYBE IT WAS JUST THE CROWDS WE ASSOCIATED WITH. MAYBE THEY WERE BAD INFLUENCES.
MAN, IT'S HOT IN THIS.
SO, WHERE ARE THE CHICKS?
CHICKS? WHAT CHICKS?
NINJA KYLE
Y'KNOW, THE CHICKS, MAN.
THE CUTE BLONDE AND THE FOXY GIRL WITH THE LUMPY HAIR.
ME AND ED ARE GONNA MAKE 'EM NINJAS.
OH, YOU ARE, ARE YOU?
LISTEN, BUCKO, THEY'RE ALREADY IN MY CLUB, AND THEY ARE NOT JOINING YOURS.
TAKE IT EASY.
I WILL NOT! YOU THINK YOU'RE MISTER COOL NINJA GUY AND EVERYONE DOES WHAT YOU SAY. BUT NOT THOSE GIRLS, BUDDY. THEY LISTEN TO ME!
AS A MATTER OF FACT, I HAVE THEM WRAPPED AROUND MY FINGER.
YOU WANT AN ARCH-ENEMY? YOU GOT IT. BUT I WILL NOT LET THOSE GIRLS JOIN YOUR CLUB! NOW SCRAM. CUZ WHEN THEY COME OUT HERE, IT'S SUPERHERO...
...TIME.

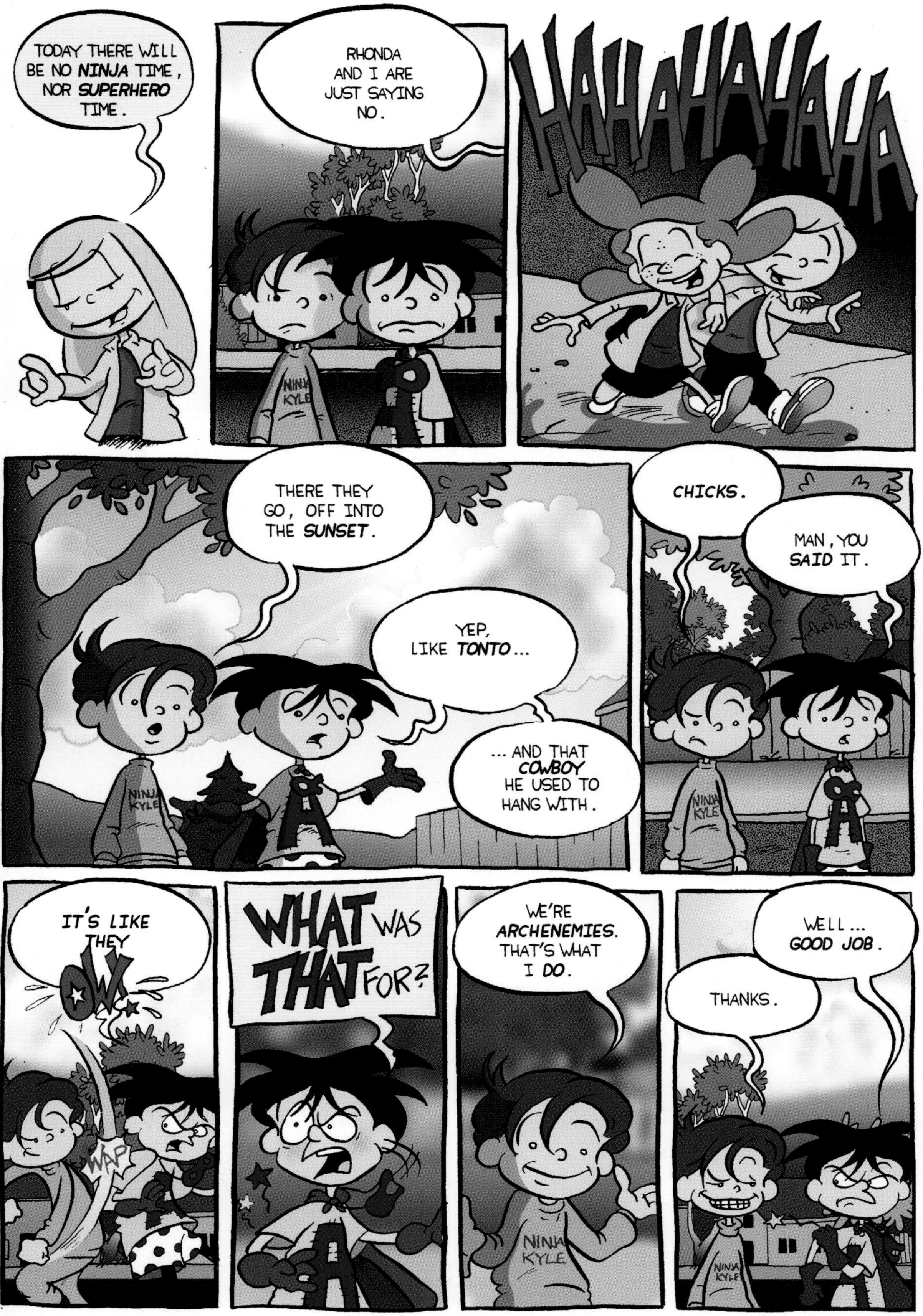
TODAY THERE WILL BE NO NINJA TIME, NOR SUPERHERO TIME.
RHONDA AND I ARE JUST SAYING NO.
HAHAHAHAHAHA
THERE THEY GO, OFF INTO THE SUNSET.
YEP, LIKE TONTO...
... AND THAT COWBOY HE USED TO HANG WITH.
CHICKS.
MAN, YOU SAID IT.
IT'S LIKE THEY
OW!
WAP
WHAT WAS THAT FOR?
WE'RE ARCHENEMIES. THAT'S WHAT I DO.
WELL... GOOD JOB.
THANKS.

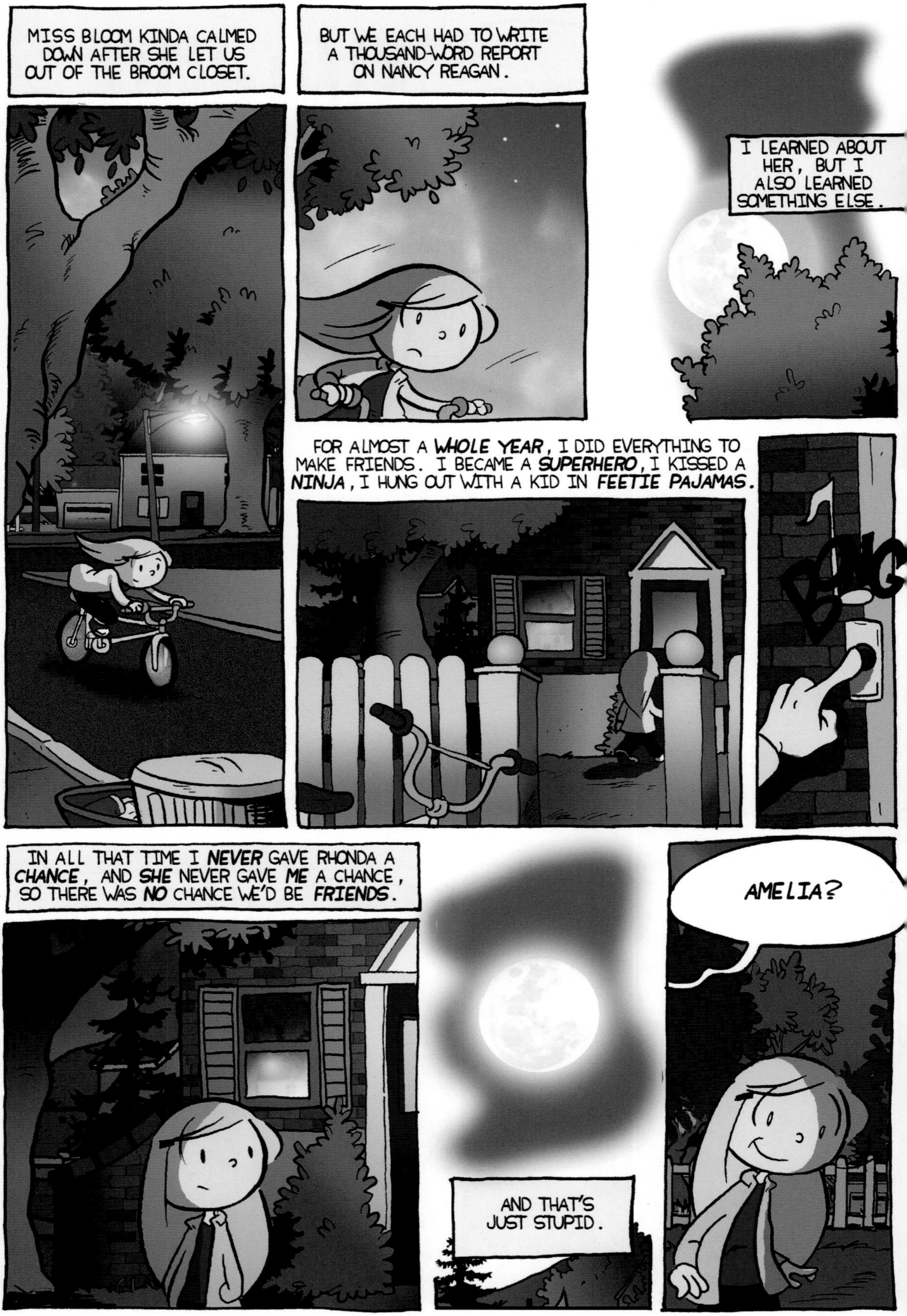
MISS BLOOM KINDA CALMED DOWN AFTER SHE LET US OUT OF THE BROOM CLOSET.
BUT WE EACH HAD TO WRITE A THOUSAND-WORD REPORT ON NANCY REAGAN.
I LEARNED ABOUT HER, BUT I ALSO LEARNED SOMETHING ELSE.
FOR ALMOST A WHOLE YEAR, I DID EVERYTHING TO MAKE FRIENDS. I BECAME A SUPERHERO, I KISSED A NINJA, I HUNG OUT WITH A KID IN FEETIE PAJAMAS.
BONG
IN ALL THAT TIME I NEVER GAVE RHONDA A CHANCE, AND SHE NEVER GAVE ME A CHANCE, SO THERE WAS NO CHANCE WE'D BE FRIENDS.
AND THAT'S JUST STUPID.
AMELIA?

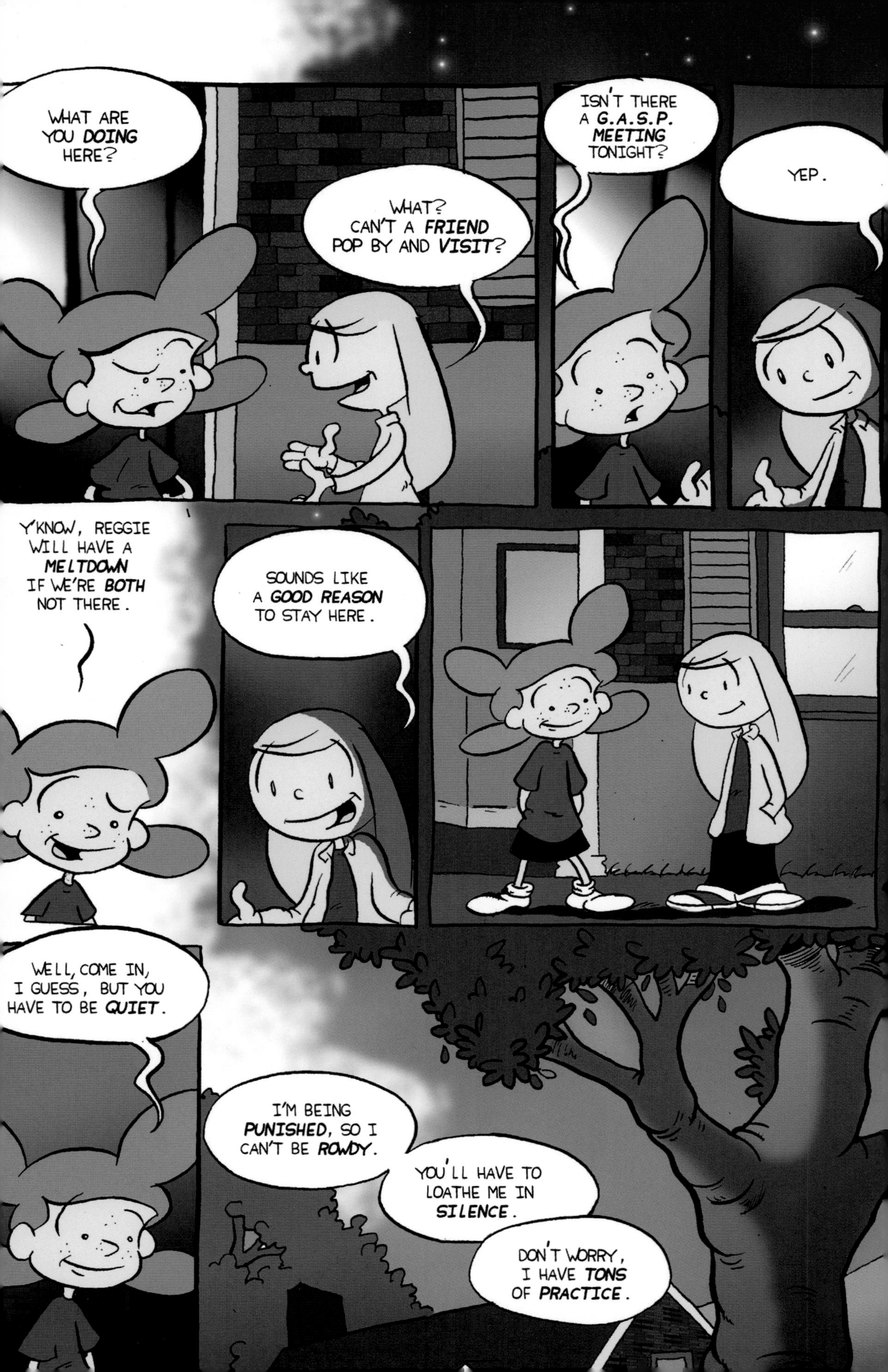
WHAT ARE YOU DOING HERE?
WHAT? CAN'T A FRIEND POP BY AND VISIT?
ISN'T THERE A G.A.S.P. MEETING TONIGHT?
YEP.
Y'KNOW, REGGIE WILL HAVE A MELTDOWN IF WE'RE BOTH NOT THERE.
SOUNDS LIKE A GOOD REASON TO STAY HERE.
WELL, COME IN, I GUESS, BUT YOU HAVE TO BE QUIET.
I'M BEING PUNISHED, SO I CAN'T BE ROWDY.
YOU'LL HAVE TO LOATHE ME IN SILENCE.
DON'T WORRY, I HAVE TONS OF PRACTICE.

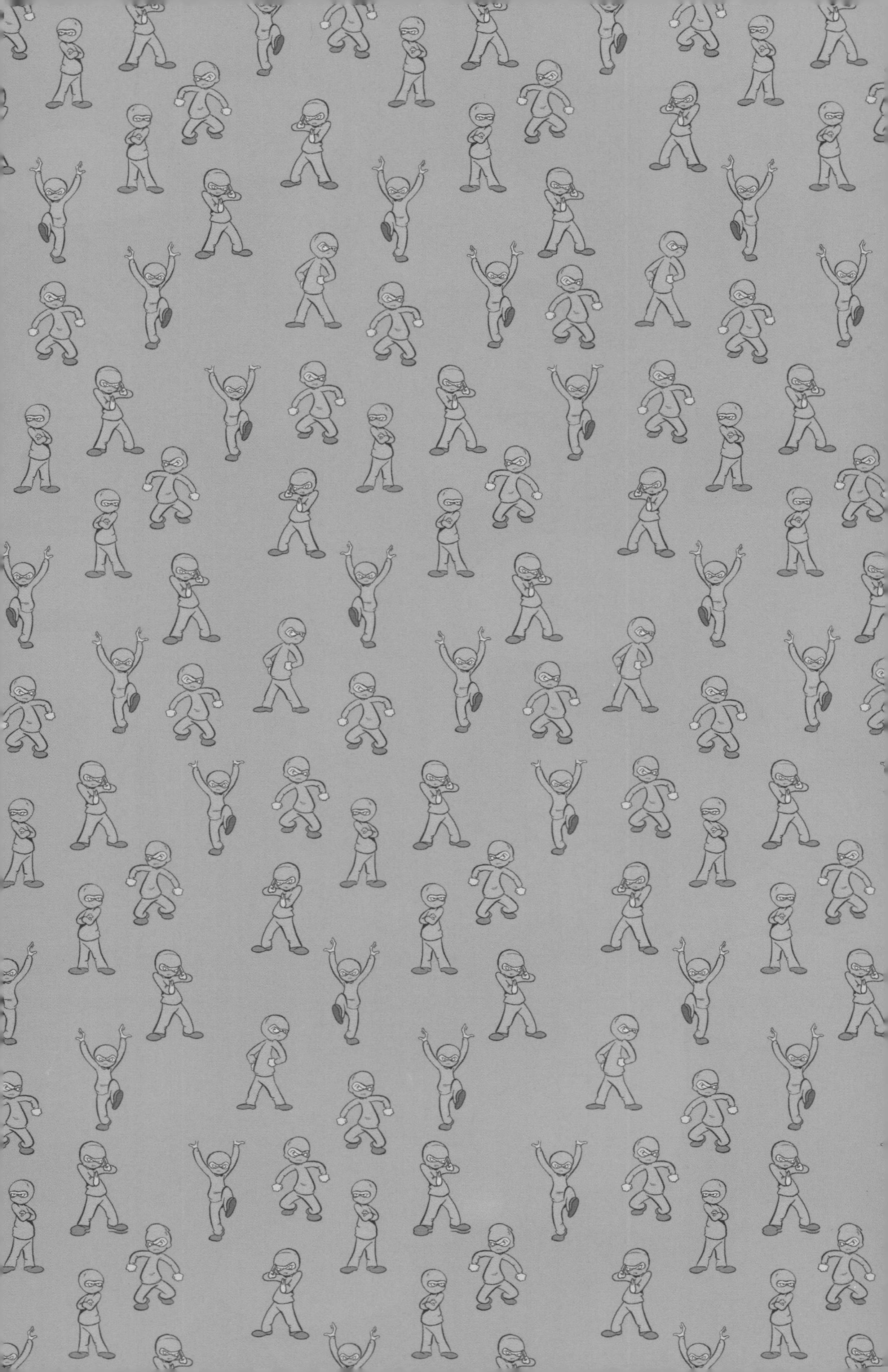

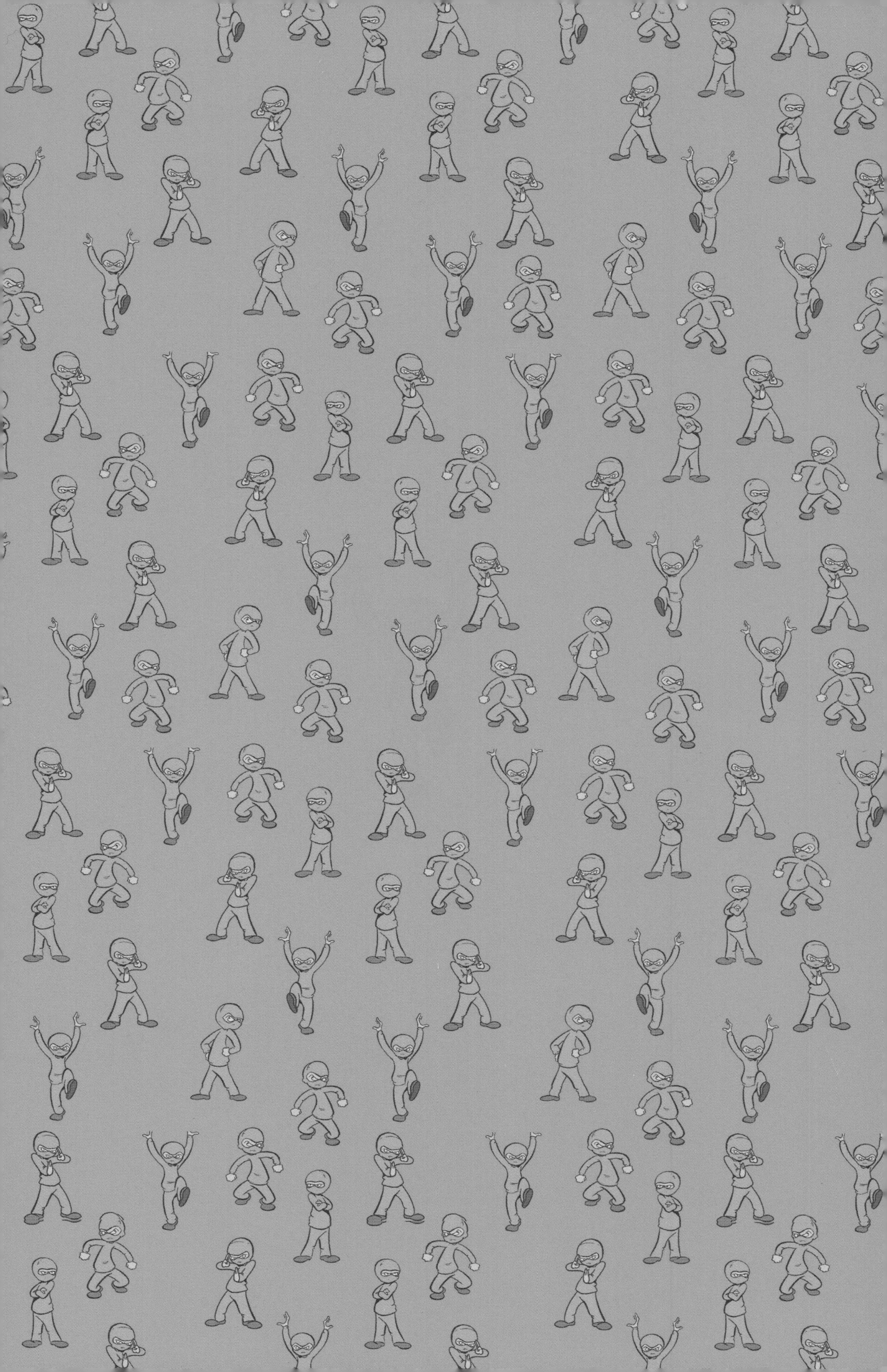